Unethical *or* Not

her life, her career and her unborn child in jeopardy

Romance* Love* Science* Law* Politics* Medicine* Change* R &D

Segun Babatunde

OLUWASEGUN, BABATUNDE

UNETHICAL OR NOT

COPYRIGHT

DEDICATION

This work is dedicated to every Nigerian that hopes for jollof rice at the end of every *owambe*. The unglamorous state of the country is energy-zapping. We therefore must **#EndSARS** and **#RestructureNigeria.**

ACKNOWLEDGEMENT

Gratitude to my late grandma: **Mrs.Feyisayo BABATUNDE**, *who instilled in me strength in the face of adversity, love in the face of hate, kindness in the face of hurt, and hard work in the face of hardship.*

Special shout out to **Evelyne BERTRAND** *(Belgium),* **Dr. Greta VERHEYEN** *(Belgium) and* **Karen SCHNAUFFER** *(United Kingdom). They are wonderful people.*

1.Initium

"A paradigm shift often starts with one act of defiance."

1. Initium

"A paradigm shift often starts with one act of defiance."

10:05 AM
Tuesday 4th February, 2025

"Dr. Ajenifuja, please, take the floor and proceed with jury selection. We have fifty persons drawn from the Southeast, Southwest, Southsouth and the Middle Belt parts of Nigeria. All from diverse professional backgrounds," Judge Ikenna Amaradi said, breaking the silence that plagued the courtroom.

"We did not include individuals from Northern Nigeria in this process since they have a different legal framework-*Sharia law*," the Judge continued, his hands under his chin. He looked at me with evident compassion.

"Dr. Adeola Jemima Ajenifuja, I know how much you have gone through in everything that has led to today. I apologise for the police harassment. I pray and hope, from here on, you shall feel safe and I also hope you will trust the process to be fair."

He turned to the prosecutor and said, "Lead Prosecutor Tundu Wada Gida, I dissuade you from your shenanigans in the media. That is unfair and unprofessional. I hereby issue a gag order, so my courtroom doesn't turn into a popular TV show. This is someone's life on the line and playing fair should be the hallmark of your practice." Gida nodded, and Judge Amaradi signaled me to proceed to the floor of the courtroom.

My legs froze with trepidation as I walked to the middle. I looked at the fifty potential jurors who sat in rows of chairs. I smiled a wan smile at them as they gazed at my protruding belly. I could stand all day and they would remain fascinated by my belly. I took a few seconds to clear my throat and began my introduction.

"My name is Dr. Adeola Jemima Ajenifuja. I am a gynaecologist and a law-abiding Nigerian. I am representing myself in these legal proceedings. Today's activity is simple and straightforward."

I moved closer to the potential jurors by the Judge's right; their eyes remained fixated on my belly, and I wondered if they had not seen a pregnant woman before.

"I'm going to use some questions to choose the fairest of you as jurors in this case," I stated. "This case could result in my losing everything I have worked for and possibly land me in jail. Most importantly, I could lose my unborn child."

The crowd murmured.

"So, if you're excused based on the questions I shall ask, please, do not take it personally. I am simply trying to ensure we have good representatives for today and tomorrow's Nigeria. Representatives who are expected to be fair."

Gida interrupted me—"My lord, Dr. Ajenifuja is pushing it too far; it's as if she is campaigning for an office or delivering a political manifesto. Her selection could be to pick for herself only the jurors who align with her position. Or even more, no one could be left after she is done."

"Please, ask your questions and make this fast," the Judge calmly urged me on, as if persuaded by my gaze upon him at his high seat.

"Here is my first question to you all," I said, and turned in the direction of the potential jurors. "Does any of you have reservations about human cloning?"

Twenty-three hands went up.

I turned to the Judge and asked in a calm tone if he could remove the jurors who raised their hands. Mr. Gida did not object, so the Judge gave approval. We had twenty-seven persons left. The intent behind this question was to evaluate the ethical concerns of the audience, using one of the most extreme embryonic manipulation techniques as a yardstick.

Thus, came my next question: "To what length would you go for your best friends to keep their memories alive even if it means going unconventional?"

"What is 'going unconventional'?" a juror asked.

I moved closer to her and said, "Going unconventional means taking a course of action that society deems wrong which isn't illegal."

She nodded her comprehension with an affirming smile.

But ten jurors raised their hands. "If it feels wrong, even without a law, it is indeed wrong," they all agreed.

I strolled towards Gida and asked the Judge to let those ten jurors go. Gida disagreed, but obliged eventually.

My next question was about the Nigerian Special Anti-Robbery Squad, popularly called SARS. "Are SARS officers beneficial to our society or not? If yes, please, raise your hand."

The four jurors who said SARS operatives were beneficial were let go. Gida shrugged when Judge Amaradi looked in his direction. He did not seem perturbed or moved by the outcome of this question.

Then we had one juror left to let go from the remaining thirteen.

I did not like the demeanour of a particular juror, a young woman with a disinterested air. And I asked for her to be removed. She stood up and headed for the door. But the Judge asked her to sit down. He sought Mr. Gida's verdict about her. "Let her go, my Lord" Gida said.

Judge Amaradi thanked everyone and said we were done for the day and adjourned the court to 18th February, 2025. We had two weeks to prepare ourselves. I caught my mother's reassuring smile in the courtroom, and strength and hope coursed through my body.

"A jury selection is a Hail Mary; you can only be hopeful."

THE COURTHOUSE

As the Judge walked out of the courtroom into his chambers, I reflected on my trip to the courthouse earlier in the day. How easy this first stage turned out to be compared to my apprehensive state when I walked into the court building that morning and felt its walls close up on me.

The streets to the courthouse were paved—they extended into the compound. A fountain was to the left, by the north gate of the compound. There were small running taps at each corner of the building utilised by the gardeners for watering the flowers. I looked up at the gigantic edifice: it reached into the heavens like the Tower of Babel. There were lifts to move up and down its high rise; and there was also a ramp for the disabled.

I made my way to the first floor where I was scheduled to appear for juror selection in Court Room 105. Last week, Dino Omolaiye, the popular *Fuji-singing* senator, was carried on a stretcher into that same floor, with braces around his neck.

I entered Court Room 105 and walked to the front, standing at the table designated for the defendant, and tried not to miss anything in this room where my fate would be given up to an altar of trials. I looked at the Judge's seat. Behind it was boldly written: "THE LAW IS THE ONLY ADVOCATE THE INNOCENT HAVE." At the table in front of the witness stand was a **Bible**, a **Quran** and an **Axe of Sango**.

The courtroom was painted in mahogany reddish-brown, the furniture clean and neatly arranged. It was highly computerised, with an AI system that monitored activities.

Nigeria had undergone an indelible metamorphosis under the leadership of its democratic President, Are-Ona Kankan-Afo. He defeated the incumbent

President Ranka Dede Bubu, a former military general who died after losing power. President Ranka Dede Bubu was suspected to have been killed by a herd of cows in his precious cattle ranch.

President Are-Ona Kankan-Afo turned the country around within a year with over £300 billion recovered from the loot of former dictator Gen. Sanni Abacha.

My case was one of those cases still unsolved at the eve of Are-Ona Kankan-Afo's administration. Now, the justice system is fair. Bribery of judges is highly unthinkable, now a thing for donkeys, giving the public confidence in the Nigerian justice system. Also, Nigerian justice system had morphed into a jury-verdict delivery system.

I will be spending some months in this courtroom fighting for my medical licence and my unborn child, and possibly seeking justice for my murdered friend, Engr. Chukwuemeka Titus Pahoose.

My mind levitated as I settled in and I was lost in thoughts. Someone called my name from behind.

"Dr. Ajenifuja! Dr. Ajenifuja." The familiar voice cut through my musings. It was my legal counsel. On her face was a genuine smile that defused my anxiety. She arrived early, too.

"Barrister Olabamiji," I answered.

She laughed as she hugged me from the side. I instinctively wrapped my hand around my growing belly and caressed her face.

We still had an hour before the court session. I sat by the aisle, as I didn't want to feel claustrophobic during the proceedings while she sat next to me. I turned to see her beautiful smile, which greeted me one more time. She said, Good morning, and I responded by saying, "Good morning Ms. Suzanna Olabamiji." Since she called me Dr. Ajenifuja despite my telling her several times to simply call me Adeola, I decided to keep calling her Ms. Olabamiji or Barrister Olabamiji. She accepted the formality.

This morning, she looked elegant in her barrister gown, a relic from our colonial masters, dear old England. Tendrils of her hairstyle through her barrister wig fell on her back. She loved making neat cornrows and favoured all-back—*patewo* or *shuku* hair styles.

"How are you doing today, Dr. Ajenifuja?"

"I am ready to do this," I said.

"I still feel it's not too late for me to stand in your defence. All I need to do is inform the court clerk about the change. It's not a complicated process," she said.

I smiled to reassure her that I understood her point. "I hired you to help me with some technicalities and legal jargons. Is there anyone in this world who can make a more convincing argument than I can on this matter? Who can see through the state's allegations better than I, uh?"

"You are the best marksman to fight your battle, even in a foreign arena."

Ms. Olabamiji nodded her agreement. She glanced at the entrance of Court Room 105 and beamed, which made me look in the same direction. I saw my parents walk into the courtroom, and I stood up to meet them halfway. My mother hugged me sweetly and my father rubbed my back.

My mother released herself from me and playfully touched my belly. "Well done, Adeola. I am so proud of you. We are very proud of you for pursuing what you believe. We are one hundred percent behind you. Iwalewa will also be here before the proceeding begins," she said.

My father stood smiling as mother rubbed my belly some more. I smiled at him, too. Then we all sat down.

Soon the courtroom filled up. By the right were the lead prosecutor for the state and the Pahoose family, who sued me for medical malpractice and for unsanctioned use of collected sperm from their deceased son. They also demanded the termination of my pregnancy—their unborn grandchild that resulted from the usage of the sperm cells. Their interest in the case was sentimental and religious, different from the state's filing against me. They claimed my actions were a sacrilege that peeved *Amadioha*. I had to be chastised, to atone for my sin by having everything stripped from me. I wondered why they didn't give this task to *Amadioha* whom I offended; instead they came to court. But they misunderstood my burden and had a different vantage to see the reason for what I did. They didn't even know I could upend the legal system in this country with the trial.

A regurgitation of my days in medical school came rushing back at that moment and disturbed me. I was an expert in cadaver dissection. I did more than needed because I found pleasure in improving my surgical skills on cadavers even though my classmates were squeamish; I never withheld my indulgent passion. For that, I was nicknamed *"Cadaver Gurl."*

I hope those records were not available to the prosecutor. I hope they won't be used as evidence against me during my trial.

My name is Adeola Jemima Ajenifuja and this is my story.

"Nigeria is a crime scene, she is a pandemic away from total extinction."

2. Cross Examination

> " A cross examination is like plucking ripe fruits in a garden. Your goal is to take home tasty fruits, but along with them, you collect some unsavoury ones. "

2. Cross Examination

"A cross examination is like plucking ripe fruits in a garden. Your goal is to take home tasty fruits, but along with them, you collect some unsavoury ones."

9:00 AM
Tuesday, 18ᵗʰ February, 2025

LA FAMILIA

My younger brother Iwalewa was the first to step out of the car, followed by my mother. My father drove them to the courthouse, parked at the parking lot, and they all walked towards me.

Iwalewa got to me first, with a countenance of guilt. He wasn't at my first court appearance and missed the jury selection. I embraced him and told him it was okay. I still love you, I said, teasing him like we always do to each other.

"Can you ever stop loving me?" he quizzed. We both laughed.

My mother met us and gently collected me off Iwalewa's hug. "Leave my baby that has another baby inside her alone," she said. My father joined her and gave me a peck on my cheek. I struggled for air as their hugs compressed me a bit. They noticed this and released me.

Our parents created lasting memories with us and taught us how to love unconditionally. When we were children, they tasked Iwalewa and I to keep piggybanks. Anytime we had visitors who gave us money, or when our uncles and aunties gave us money, we kept it in our piggy banks. By year end, we broke the piggybanks and, even if I had ₦2,000 and Iwalewa had ₦500, we were asked to buy gifts with each person's savings for each other. It was hard to accept that all our savings for the year went to the other person, but we were eventually accustomed to it as an expression of love.

In my adolescence, my family and I went to Mr. Bigg's restaurant and I saw a homeless man at the entrance. We had gone for Boxing Day celebration and planned to break our piggybanks after the lunch. While we sat at the table, my father went to place our orders at the counter. I spoke softly to my mother.

"Did you see that man near the entrance, the homeless man?"

"Yes, why?" she answered.

"Why don't we gift our money this year to that homeless man instead? He seems to need it more," I said.

My mother paused for some seconds, tears rolling down her face. She embraced me tightly and cried even more. Father arrived at this time with our orders on a tray. He was flustered. When he learnt what happened, he was moved.

My parents suggested that instead of giving the entire savings to the man, we should buy him provisions and food. Iwalewa and I nodded in agreement, so we decided to order some food from the counter for him. He was later provided with new clothes and supplies.

"When groomed from the cradle to make sacrifices, big-heartedness becomes a norm in adulthood."

*   *   *

THE FIRST WITNESS

We eventually entered the courtroom and I sat close to my legal counsel. My family sat behind us. The session was going to start in thirty minutes and we were eager.

"Sis," Iwalewa called, fear in his voice, "I am nervous. What if? . . ."

"I am not afraid of the worst, *bruh*. Let's be positive," I said to him.

Mr. Gida, the lead prosecutor, and the Pahoose family sat ready on the right side of the courtroom.

The clerk announced our case number, ABJ/2024/COURT105/CASE008.

Judge Amaradi ordered the bailiff, Mr. Omolola Aguntasolo, to bring in the jury, who proceeded to the jurors' benches, two rows each row for six persons. The jury was balanced with six men and six women.

The defence—myself, and the lead prosecutor gave brief opening statements.

Judge Amaradi gave the floor to LP Gida to bring in his first witness to take an oath.

"I hereby call to witness, Dr. Etti Ikemefuna from the Coroner's Office of Abuja Area Council Hospital," said Mr. Gida.

The bailiff brought in Dr. Ikemefuna who was asked to enter the witness box. Dr. Ikemefuna was a traditionalist, so he took his oath with **Sango's Axe**. Hence,

LP Gida began his cross-examination of Dr. Ikemefuna.

"Good morning. My name is Mr. Tundun Wada Gida. I am from the Prosecutor's Office. How are you today, sir?" he asked genially.

"I am fine, thank you," Dr. Ikemefuna answered.

Mr. Gida paused before asking his next questions.

"Please, can you give us one, your full name; two, your credentials; three, your present position; and four, what your job entails?"

"Well, my name is Dr. Etti Ikemefuna. I obtained my bachelor's degree in Medicine and Surgery from Obafemi Awolowo University, Ile Ife. I proceeded to Cambridge University in the UK for a master's in Forensic Archaeology and Anthropology. I am presently the Director-in-Charge, Coroner's Office of Abuja Area Council Hospital." He took a deep breath and looked the way of the jury before he continued. "My job is to conduct autopsies, that is, to examine corpses and determine the cause of death and any related issues observable on a dead body."

"Thank you, Dr. Ikemefuna," LP Gida said briskly. "Is it true you received the corpse of Engr. Chukwuemeka Pahoose on 10th August 2023, roughly eighteen months ago? What were your observations?"

"Yes, I indeed received Engr. Pahoose's body on the said date. There were two gunshots to his chest. He died instantly. Dr. Adeola Adenifuja accompanied the body to my morgue. At the time, everything seemed intact as we immediately removed all the clothes and personal effects of Engr. Pahoose and bagged them accordingly," Dr. Ikemefuna answered.

"You didn't suspect foul play at the time?" Mr. Gida asked.

"Not at all. I excused myself to get some chemical reagent from the lab and returned ten minutes later. I discovered something missing from the body. It was the whole scrotum. It was surgically removed. The testicles were gone. We searched for Dr. Ajenifuja but she had disappeared."

"Thank you, Dr. Ikemefuna for such details," Mr. Gida said. He looked at the jury then asked the coroner his next question.

"Has anything like this happened before under your watch?"

"No, certainly not."

"So, how did Dr. Ajenifuja have such access and freedom in your domain?"

"Well, Dr. Ajenifuja works in the same hospital complex as I and her access card gave her access to our section. After checking with IT, it was revealed that she accessed my workstation. It appears she was the only one who was there within those ten minutes I was away."

"Thank you, Dr. Ikemefuna. I will allow the defence to cross-examine you."

"Your Honour, her witness," Gida ended and returned to his seat.

"Dr. Adeola Ajenifuja, your witness," Judge Amaradi said to me.

I stood up and asked my first question.

"Was that the only time this incident has happened in your workstation, Dr. Ikemefuna? And, please, be reminded, you are under oath."

He exhaled before answering, "Well there was a report of such incident in the past, where a whole body got missing. This was before my employment at the Coroner's Office."

"Thank you for that clarification," I said.

I moved from my seat and walked towards him.

"So, what was the previous investigation like? I assume you have read the file?"

Giwa cut in. "Objection, Your Honour! Your Honour, Dr. Ikemefuna was not in employment at this time and cannot give details of an incident that happened before he was employed at this office."

Judge Amaradi overruled the objection: "I will allow it. I will give a little latitude."

So, Dr. Ikemefuna explained that from the content of the file, there was a system glitch and a body for examination was tagged for cremation. Therefore, the investigation of the homicide could not be carried out.

I was happy with this information. It proved the system was not fool-proof, and it was a piece of information I wanted the jury to hear.

I excused Dr. Ikemefuna and began to plot my next move.

Judge Amaradi adjourned the court till the next day.

OUR HOME

After my first cross-examination of Dr. Etti Ikemefuna in court, I went home with my parents and Iwalewa. My parents own a beautiful house in Maitama, Abuja, which my friends call a mansion because of its palatial look.

My father is a renowned professor of chemistry at the University of Abuja, but his fortune came from "Olamol," a synthetic analgesic that was a phenomenal success more than twenty years ago.

He discovered and owned the original patent for the drug, which he sold to Smithscon Pharmaceuticals and made a huge fortune which several Ajenifuja generations will keep benefitting from for a long time.

In his contract with Smithscon Pharmaceuticals, he named the invention after his first child, me. The drug was named Olamol(*"Ola"* from Adeola), the most powerful painkiller invented without any side effects or addictive influence. He never got to invent another product. He probably would have named it after Iwalewa. And what name that would have been for a drug in the market, especially the international market. "Iwalewa," sounds mouthful, does it not? I imagine my father inventing a gas substance, he would have chosen a name relative to hydrogen or oxygen and name it "Iwalegen" or, if it was a member of the halogen family such as Chlorine, Fluorine, Bromine or Iodine, it probably would have been "Iwalerine."

HIS WITNESS

It was mother's regular check-up with her endocrinologist, and she was scheduled for 9:00 AM on 19th February 2025. She was diabetic. So, she and my father came late to the court because of her check-up with the doctor. Iwalewa and I headed for the court in my car.

On my way, I got a surprise WhatsApp message from my friend Jumoke Olagunju. She asked me to send her the direction to the courthouse. Jumoke lived in Liverpool, United Kingdom; what did she need the direction to the court in Abuja for? I wondered. I sent it to her anyway.

When I arrived at the court, she was waiting for us. She came miles away to be with me in my tribulation. My eyes welled up with tears when I saw her. She hugged me warmly and told me I would be fine. She was such a sweet friend. I missed her fiercely when she moved to the United Kingdom to continue her medical studies. She followed my case from the UK and always gave her emotional support from the beginning. But finding her here this morning was heart-warming.

Three of us went into the courtroom where my counsel was already waiting. I sat in the first row, with Jumoke and Iwalewa behind me. The court session began some minutes after, and Mr. Gida called me to the stand as his next witness.

I objected but Judge Amaradi overruled it. He said I was on the list of witnesses and since I already knew this, I had to comply. My counsel nodded and I went to the stand to take my oath. I swore with a Bible as a Christian.

"Good morning, Dr. Adenifuja," Mr. Gida greeted me.

"Good morning, Mr. Gida."

"Can you kindly give the court the following details: one, your full name; two, your profession; three, your place of employment; and four, years of work?"

My eyes roamed the courtroom; Iwalewa and Jumoke looked like cheerleaders. I felt the collective gaze of the jurors zoom in on me. I responded.

"My name is Adeola Jemima Adenifuja, I am a gynaecologist at Abuja Area Council Hospital. I work in the IVF wing of the Department of Reproductive Medicine. I have been with the department for three years."

"Is it safe to say you are an expert in the field of Reproductive Science?" Mr. Gida asked.

"You can say that!"

"Who is Engr. Chukwuemeka Pahoose and what is your relationship with him, Dr. Ajenifuja?"

"Engr. Chukwuemeka Titus Pahoose was my best friend before his life was cut-short by officers of the SARS police unit."

"My condolences, Dr. Ajenifuja, and apologies for such avoidable death of your friend."

He gave me a few minutes to be prepared for his next questions.

"For perspective, I would like to borrow your expertise as a doctor in the field of Reproductive Medicine, can you tell this court how long sperm cells can survive in a dead person? A dead man, so to speak?" Mr. Gida clarified.

I waited a few more seconds to gather my thoughts.

"It is optimal to retrieve sperm cells from the epididymis, the storage part of the testes, within twenty-four hours. But it can also be done successfully within thirty-six hours."

"About eighteen months ago, you arrived with the lifeless body of your friend Engr. Pahoose at Dr. Etti Ikemefuna's morgue. Ten minutes after, the scrotum of the corpse was missing. You're a resident gynaecologist with a bachelor's degree in medicine and surgery and have valuable years of experience in reproductive medicine. It is on record that you used your card to access and exit the morgue within the ten minutes of Dr. Ikemefuna's exit from his lab. Is it safe to say you actually removed the scrotum of your dead friend Engr. Pahoose?" Mr. Gida asked. "Did you loot his testes?" he asked again, assertively.

"Yes," I said.

"Yes, what? Be specific, Dr. Adenifuja."

"Yes, I was responsible for the missing scrotum. I finely removed the scrotum, opened his scrotal sac, collected sperm cells and cryopreserved them," I said sternly.

"It is fascinating how a dead man can father a child within thirty-six hours of dying.

But rather than fanfare for medical science and those using it for a befitting purpose, we have a jury."

A loud cry from the right side of the courtroom disrupted the quietness of our space. It came from Engr. Pahoose's mother. A strong murmur rose from the jury.

Judge Amaradi slammed his gavel to maintain order in his courtroom.

After order returned, Mr. Gida asked his last question. "Did you get pregnant from the retrieved sperm cell of deceased Engr. Pahoose?"

"Yes," I whispered.

"I didn't catch that," Mr. Gida enquired.

"Yes!" I shouted and supressed myself from bursting into tears.

Members of the Pahoose family stood up and began to shout. A portion of the jury swelled and tilted in my direction with grave concern.

"No further questions, Your Honour," Mr. Gida said as he turned to go back to his seat. "Dr. Ajenifuja can step off the witness stand."

My legs felt heavier as I walked away from the stand.

The Judge adjourned the court till next Wednesday. Myself and my folks and supporters were demoralised.

"I was not going to lie under oath and perjure myself. Besides I had my strategy and I am going to apply it the next time," I said to Iwalewa, who hugged me when I returned to my seat.

"A witness stand is not like a confession: you cannot choose what you tell"

We left the court and Jumoke said we should go to Mr. Bigg's to have fun and forget about the day.

My name is Adeola Jemima Ajenifuja, and this is my story.

"THE LAW IS THE ONLY ADVOCATE THE INNOCENT HAVE"

3. The Ajenifujas

> " The cleaving together of two **'matters'** of differing atomic numbers and weights to become one chemical entity is a paradox, a light year away from full comprehension."

3. The Ajenifujas

"The cleaving together of two 'matters' of differing atomic numbers and weights to become one chemical entity is a paradox, a light year away from full comprehension."

ORDERED STEPS

I sat in the living room and tried to take my mind off the case by flipping through TV channels for something interesting when mother walked in.

"Are you good?" my mother asked and caressed my shoulder gently.

I sighed and nodded. She smiled and sat beside me on the sofa.

"This world is such an interesting place. I was scrolling through Facebook and, on the 'People You May Know' column, was a person I knew from my days in Jos around the time I met your father. The man looked much older than I expected."

"Why was he looking old, Mum? Was he ill?" I asked.

I did not press to know, she said.

Then suddenly she laughed and said, "I have forgotten how much time had passed since those days your father gave me sleepless nights."

"Your epic love story," I joked.

"Yes indeed, our love story has been an epic journey that shows no signs of slowing down."

I sat up and turned to her, "Tell me how you met Daddy. I'm badly in need of a distraction."

My mother smiled, drew closer, started patting my hair, then began:

YEAR 1997

"I met your father while working as a secretary at one of the firms at the Murtala Mohammed building in Jos. He came to my office to get his research proposal typed. He was the new chemical analyst at the pharmaceutical company adjacent to our office. The name of the company was Berom Central Pharmacy, Murtala Mohammed Way, Jos. He had much typing to do and I had some hours of spare time, so I offered to do part of the typing for him while he did the other part.

"While I typed his work, I noticed some grammatical and syntactic errors. I discussed them with him, and he was charmed by my brilliance. He said he was impressed. I brushed that aside, though I was pleased with his compliments.

"We started and finished the work that day. I handed over the finished work to him and he asked me how he could show gratitude for my help. I told him not to worry, that his pleasant attitude and his compliments were enough thanks.

'I wish you all the best in this research and hope it helps people,' I said as he stood up to leave.

'So, you understand my project?' he asked with surprise on his face.

'Well, not exactly. But your abstract gave me a glimpse of the whole idea. You are trying to find a safer and cheaper analgesic without any contraindication or adverse effect,' I said, while I picked up my bag for the day.

"I walked him to the door and looked around the office to be sure I hadn't forgotten anything.

'Wow! You're really impressive,' he said, then asked for my name. I told him, Oludayo Yusuf.

He wanted to tell his name, but I already beat him to it. 'I know your name, Femi Akinrinola Ajenifuja.'

'How did you know my name?'

'I just typed eighty per cent of your research work, remember? And, by the way, who puts the names of his unborn children in a dedication page?' I asked him.

"By that time, we were across the road from the Murtala Mohammed building and we walked at a leisurely pace. I wanted to get some *akara* from the woman across the road. The woman had been a lifesaver since I joined the company as a secretary. Her *akara* was my main meal in the evenings and it gave me more time to relax after work, instead of spending precious time making meals for only one mouth.

"'I have always dreamed of having four kids, and what better way than to pray it into life? I have reserved Adeola, Iwalewa, Shunamite and Onígègé Àrà in Heaven's register,' he said with so much confidence.

'I hope you know you'll need your partner's input and consent on the number of kids you want and their names? You are not an alpha on those,' I told him as I paid five naira for a full nylon bag of *akara* from the woman.

'Well, I do. I hope my God-sent partner compromises in my favour, if not, we will work something out. It is not cast in stone,' he said, laughing in a way that suggested that if he had such discussions with his partner, he would be the person likely to compromise.

"I sat on one of the woman's benches and asked him to sit beside me. I was enjoying our conversation.

He held his typed document in a folder and gently arranged it in his backpack

"Mummy, I'd like to get a glass of water. I am *kinda* thirsty," I said, interrupting Mother's engrossing autobiography. She nodded and paused, tailing me with her eyes as I walked out of the living room. I returned, sat beside her, and asked her to resume.

"So, I asked him to share the *akara* with me and he agreed; the typical hungry bachelor on the lookout for food he must have been, I thought to myself. I told him, 'Tell me why those four names matter to you. Imagine this was a sales pitch. Sell those names to me.'

He wolfed down the ball of *akara* in his hand and pulled out a bottle of water from his bag and downed it to wet his throat. He sat up and looked at me as if he was about to tell me the most sacred secret ever, as if he had been looking for an audience for a long time. His hands raised in the manner of a politician about to give a long speech.

"'The name Adéolá as you know, literally means 'A crown of *wealth*.' In Yoruba—Oh, I forgot to ask…which state you are from?' he implored, looking directly into my eyes as I gulped a cold bottle of Pepsi. 'I am from Omu-Aran in Kwara State,' I said.
'I am from Ila Orangun, in Osun state,' he replied and continued with his reasons for choosing those four names for his unborn children.

Adéolá, chosen for my first unborn child, strikes a chord in me. The pronunciation is *'Her-day-holla*. I wanted a name related to kingship, a name affiliated with royalty affluence and wealth. Adeola seems to be the choicest based on this idea. Ìwàlewà, the name for my second unborn child was chosen because I don't believe that outward beauty is enough. Iwalewa's literal meaning is *'Good character is the real beauty.'*

"By then, I finished my *akara* and Pepsi and clapped to his pitch. We both walked away from the *akara* shop and, as we strolled to the bus stop, he asked if he could continue his speech to explain the other two names.
'Tell me about them,' I urged him.
'I first heard the name *'Shunamite'* on a radio programme. It was the name of a caller. It sounded nice to me. I researched and found out it was a name in the Bible and I loved it even more.'
'What about the other name, the Yoruba one?" I asked.

Onígègé Àrà means *'Someone whose pen writes wonders.'* Someone capable of penning down ingenious ideas and achieving great feats,' he said passionately.
'So, who is the lucky woman to accept this proposal for unborn children?' I asked.
He looked at me and said, 'You.'

"I laughed hysterically for, at least, two minutes.
'You don't even know me. You don't know my middle name nor my last name. Do you know if I'm a serial killer or *Karishika*? What if I am a

psycho who escaped Aro Psychiatric Hospital, Lagos and moved up to Jos to start over?'

'Wow! I'm very scared. I need to leave now. I have never heard someone pitch themselves in such scary details. I am so frightened, scared for my life even,' he said while gesticulating his fright. Then he took his turn to laugh. I kicked him for successfully dramatizing a fake fear.

"At the bus stop, as I was about to flag a taxi, he stopped laughing, looked at me soberly and said softly in his baritone voice: 'Nobody really knows anybody. Relationships are sometimes a game of luck. Like a bet. An attempt in Las Vegas to make some winning.'

"I was attentive at this point, so I stayed on to listen further. He continued in his soft baritone voice, a voice already winning me over. He paused and looked at me, so I nodded to show him I was following. I looked into his clean white eyes as he spoke on.

'In the end, what matters is when an opportunity comes, you give it a try. Now it is possible to play games, to toy with hearts, to be a playboy, a *Yoruba demon*. It is also possible to be a good person, a good human being. We sure will not know if we never tried, would we?'

"I nodded and smiled. I told him that his ability to engage without sweet talk or flattery was commendable. Yet, I had the feeling that he could still be an undercover *Yoruba demon*.

"He laughed again but I had flagged down a taxi. I told him I enjoyed the day with him and would like to talk another time.

'Can we see after work tomorrow?' he asked. 'We can get *akara* and Pepsi and you'll tell me all your secrets.'

'Let me check my schedule,' I teased him, and he smiled in understanding.

'Busy Madam, please, make time for me tomorrow and I promise it will be worth your while.'

"We smiled at each other as I opened the door of the taxi and slid in."

ÓLEKÚ

"I thought about him all night and fell asleep with thoughts of him. I wasn't surprised I dreamed about him.

"The next day, he was already waiting for me at the door by 4:45 PM. He leaned on the office wall, looking extremely handsome. His face showed surprise and I knew it was about my dress. I wore an aqua-coloured Ankara gown with a starburst design. My handbag was made by Bata, which was a growing Fashion brand of the time.

"The Popular Bata?" I asked my mother. "Did you know Bata brand from way back?"

"Yes, the brand has been around for a while. My shoes are equally from Bata. It was not the usual fashion trend for that era, but I knew I looked stunning," she said.

One look at your father showed that my fashion for the evening was right. He gasped in admiration. He did not look bad either. He wore a blue short-sleeved shirt and a pair of brown chinos trousers. When he said 'Hi,' my heart thumped faster. I saw his handsomeness more than I did the day before.

"He came closer and the air got fresher with his cologne. He complimented my attire and said he liked *Ankara* fabric, which was his best African fabric.

'You smell good,' I said. I wanted to say so much more—to compliment his shirt, his shoes—but I decided to take it slow.

'I like your dress and I think your sneakers are perfect. I've never seen this kind of sneakers before,' I said to him and turned to shut the office door.

'How was your day?' he asked as we walked away from the office. I told him my day went well and asked how his day had been.

'It was cool,' he answered, and we walked into the fading sunshine of the evening. 'I want us to see a movie today. My colleagues have been talking about it and calling it a must-watch.'

'What movie is that?' I asked.

"The movie's title was 'Ólekú, and I said it was okay because my friends had also seen it and commended it. I really wasn't keen on movies and hadn't seen it yet. He insisted we ate before going to see it and I agreed. I didn't want my stomach rumbling in the cinema.

"We took a taxi to a notable restaurant in Jos in the Bukuru Annex. I ordered *tuwo shinkafa* and *vegetable soup* with some bush meat and a bottle of Pepsi. I still remember what he ordered as well—pounded yam, *egusi* soup and a bottle of Malta Guinness. I don't think I can forget any detail about my life's journey with your father.

"We finished our meal and boarded a taxi to the cinema at Rayfield. Rayfield is the settlement area for elite Jos. At the cinema, we got seats in the middle row and saw Óleku The actor whose name was Ajani left little to be desired. He was a Yoruba demon, a player and manipulator of women. I detested him immediately.

"Femi and I discussed Ajani's wickedness. Your father agreed that Ajani was indeed a bad boy, but he was more impressed by the cinematography, the storytelling and the movie's plot.

"The story did not end, therefore, we had to be back to see the next instalment. I asked Femi if he was an Ajani as we stepped out of the cinema.

'No, I'm not,' he said meekly. 'I have always prayed to love one woman and I strongly believe I can.'

"Looking back now, I admit that my question was a little weird. If he was a man like Ajani, was I really expecting him to admit that to me?

"We were out of the cinema hall, walking in an open space. He pulled me by my hand, took me to a corner and said, 'I'd like to kiss you.' This man had been seeing too many American movies, I thought. But I decided to live dangerously and give Jos people something to talk about. So, I smiled and nodded. He pulled me gently and planted a kiss on my lips; he turned his head to the other side and changed the style. At first, there was no tongue contact. I placed my hand around his neck ecstatically in submission. I didn't know when I felt his tongue, which tasted like menthol and sent an electric charge down my spine.

"Then he eased himself momentarily from me and looked into my eyes with a boyish face. I looked back at him and gave him a signal to continue. We kissed for a time longer than five minutes. I felt flushed, my breasts tingled, and I felt a pool flood between my legs. I wanted more but I suppressed my desire, as I did not want to feel cheap.

"Mummy!" I shouted.

"Look at this *child o*," she answered. "Do you think it was your generation that invented dangerous living? Leave me alone *O jàre,*" she said, with a naughty smile and continued the story of her escapade with Dad.

"Back to the story, I noticed he didn't try beyond kissing even though he knew I would have let him have more of me. We disengaged and walked, holding hands, to the bus stop to get a taxi.

"I looked at my watch as we got into the taxi, it was already 9:00 PM. He said he was taking me to my house, then home afterwards. We sat, locked together like the enzyme-substrate lock-and-key phenomenon postulated by Emil Fischer in 1894.

"The ride took twenty-five minutes as the driver took the longer but more scenic route. We didn't mind that he was trying to rip us off; we enjoyed each other's company. I rested my head on your father's chest. He kissed my hair intermittently and wrapped his arms around me.

"We arrived at my house and he walked me to my door, then planted a kiss on my lips.
'See you tomorrow,' he said as he walked away into the thick darkness of Jos night.

"As usual, thoughts of him filled my head and heart throughout the night and I was falling in love.
"We saw the next day and spent each day afterwards hanging out and having lunch and dinner together; we became inseparable.

*   *   *

FETISHES AND FANTASIES

One Saturday, three months later, we decided to go to Rayfield Park. He wore a red T-shirt, a pair of blue jeans and looked more handsome. As we entered a taxi to Rayfield, I noticed he was preoccupied but I didn't dwell on it because I enjoyed placing my head on his chest.

"We were talking about buying strawberries when he suddenly said, 'Will you marry me?'

I burst into laughter and sat up closely to him.

'We are not earning much and should not start marriage yet,' I said in a sober tone.

'I'm not saying we should get married immediately, but I want you and everyone else to know that you are mine. I want to mark out my territory so that no wandering eyes and legs can invade it.'

'What! When did I become a territory?' I asked with shock in my voice.

'Well, in the animal kingdom, animals such as lizards mark their territories around their love interests, so other male lizards do not encroach. They even release pheromones to assert their position. It's just a way to tell other males off,' he answered. 'Besides, I have not given you a ring yet. I just want you to know my intention. It is not for fun. This is heartfelt.'

"I exhaled and told him that I cared for him as well and cherished his intention as I was beginning to love him. Then he asked what I loved about him.

'I like that you are moderately ambitious. I do not see greed in your desires, motivations or actions. Most people wouldn't wait around once they have a discovery of something new like your project. They would leave their jobs immediately. But you are waiting for your breakthrough before you decide what next and I like that,' I said.

'Is that all?' he asked with a naughty smile.

"I hit his shoulder playfully and he pretended to fall from the impact. How I love his playfulness; he wasn't the kind of man who took everything too seriously.

I asked him, 'Wouldn't you tell me what you like about me?'

He laughed and said he liked everything about me. Then he drew close and kissed me. My head spun. I was surprised that was his next line of action. He saw my surprised face and stopped.

"He smiled and said we should talk about sex. My surprise turned into shock—the change in conversation was so sudden.

'What do you think?' he asked. My mouth was suddenly incapable of forming words.

'I like to be clear and not assume things to ensure we are both on the same page about everything from the start. For example, I don't do anal sex.'

'Anal sex?' I cringed. 'I only use my anus to poo. I would not want anything going in,' I said, revulsion coursing through my entire body.

'I don't either,' he said and pushed his hands further inside his pockets. There was silence for about two minutes, then he spoke.

'So, we are clear on anal?'

'Yes,' I answered.

"I believe though that each couple should be left to their choices. My lack of interest in anal sex does not invalidate other people's choices.

I fairly nodded to move past the topic.

"Then we talked about missionary position, oral, sucking of breasts, squirting, doggy style, our fantasies and fetishes".

"Mummy!" I gasped. "You both were very wild! I didn't even think that people discussed sex freely in 1997."

"This girl *leave me o*," my mother answered. "Is this your story or mine? We lived our lives to the fullest back then and you know that your father and I have never been the type to pretend."

Parents can project innocence, but they were yesterday's wild youth. We have no idea what sexual ringtones fired us into existence.

Mother continued:

I told your father I squirt heavily. He smiled and said he can handle a heavy downpour. I told him my fantasy was making love on the beach while the waves crashed around us and sprayed us with water droplets. My other fantasy was to have hot, crazy sex on the topmost floor of a skyscraper.

'I can get that done,' he said.

I asked what his fetishes and fantasies were, and he stammered.

'I like fondling the boobs from behind while pounding. I love to do the two simultaneously.'

"I noted to him that what he had were fantasies. Fetishes on the other hand, somewhat, involve breaking boundaries by doing stuffs that are weird but sometimes permissible.

'That means I don't have any fetish then,' he said thoughtfully.

"It was pleasing to have that discussion. We were both comfortable chatting about things that were taboo subjects at the time. We eventually took a taxi, and, during the journey, he brought out an envelope and handed it to me.

      "It was a letter from Smithscon Pharmaceuticals, Lagos; the company had expressed interest in his project and had invited him to Lagos for a meeting the next week.

'Congratulations!' I said while hugging him, then planted a wet kiss on his lips.

We arrived at my place and he walked with me to my door. We kissed again, passionately. I was not ready to have sex that day, so I decided not to invite him in.

      "We had been together for three months, but we had never had the talk about sex until that day. The fact that we had that talk relieved us of any pressure around the subject. Yet, I chose not to go further that day. So, we said goodbye and planned to see after church the next day to hangout as he would leave for Lagos on Monday.

      "I felt anxiety as I realised that we had never been apart for even a day in three months. In such a short time, Femi had become everything to me."

*   *   *

SPUR-OF-THE-MOMENT

      "After church the next day, we went to the market to get groceries, and from there went to his place.

We made lunch. I cooked while he washed plates. I made jollof rice and *owàmbè* stew.

'Why have you never made *jollof rice* for me?' he wondered aloud.

Well, that's because you have never let me cook for you. I am even surprised you let me cook today, I answered.

He was quiet for a while. Then he said, 'I've never even thought about it. I just like to cook for my special lady when she comes around.

      "I snuggled up to him on the sofa. We watched the video of 'Dyna' by Daddy Showkey on TV.

'How did you manage to get time off work?' I asked after the song ended.

He reached for the remote and muted the TV, looked into my eyes, and his lips pursed.

'I already had an overdue vacation, so I used it. I told the office my wife was pregnant, and I needed to travel to see her.'

'What!' I screamed and sprang to my feet.

'Femi! You're married and you have been deceiving me all this while?'

Ìfé mi, calm down! I was referring to you. You are the pregnant wife,' he said in a soothing tone.

'Who is your *Ìfé*? Who is your love? It's definitely not me but your pregnant wife in Lagos,' I snapped.

"He came to me and held my waist, kissed my shoulder and apologised for getting me upset. He had only been joking and he didn't know I wouldn't see it as a joke.

'Well, I don't like that joke very much,' I said.

He pulled me into his arms and sat on the sofa; I fell onto his lap. He stroked my hair, apologised in Yoruba and whispered his affection for me. I breathed heavily. We began kissing—the kisses were fast and hot and we both knew it wasn't business as usual.

"He slipped his hand under my shirt and reached for the mound under my bra. He touched my pointing nipple and pinched it softly, then unhooked my bra.

"My lips and palms roamed all over his torso, raising his moans. I didn't know when my skirt came off. I only felt his hands gently pulling down my panties and felt current surge through me. His fingers explored and drove me crazy. I gently helped his sizeable manhood out of his boxers, then sat on him cowgirl style. He kissed my breast while I rode him. He moaned. I moaned. We climaxed. Then we went another round with me squirting heavily and Femi taking it all in.

"We showered together. By nightfall, we took a taxi to my place and he kissed me passionately at the door and said good night.

'I will come to your office by 2:00 PM tomorrow to say goodbye before heading for the airport,' he said. I nodded. When I entered my flat, my emotions were undiscernible to me; the pleasure earlier remained unforgettable.

*   *   *

FEMI IN LASGIDI

Femi was in faraway Lagos, a former capital of Nigeria. The name 'Lagos' had by this year morphed into 'Lasgidi' on the streets. He and I hadn't spoken for two days and I was getting worried, very worried. He was able to reach out eventually, and we talked briefly. His project with the pharmaceutical company progressed enough that they wanted him to travel to London.

"His work was outstanding, and the firm wanted him to replicate it with large-scale experiments. To do that required a state-of-the-art laboratory and the company decided that its sister pharmaceutical company, Smithscon Pharmaceuticals, London, was an excellent choice. An international passport and visa were quickly arranged for him and he was about to get on the plane when he asked to speak to me. Everything had happened so fast and he had no time to even catch his breath. It was one evening I got the call, as I was leaving the office.

"This happened before the GSM era and I didn't have a phone in my house, so, he couldn't call me immediately he got to his hotel in London. But when I walked into the office the next day, a caller had been waiting on the line for me. It was Femi, so excited to share with me the things he saw in London. We spoke for almost an hour.

"The company offered him a preliminary contract. They paid him an inconvenience allowance, which accompanied a daily stipend of two hundred pounds for his work in the lab. They took care, also, of his feeding and accommodation. He was very happy. He met several drug design scientists at the company who had all read about his breakthrough and were amazed at his success and brilliance in spite of the crude apparatus and lab equipment he used back home to develop the world's first general-action, non-addictive analgesic. His drug was effective for every kind of pain such as bone pain, soft tissue pain, and nerve pain and it had negligible side effects on both human and animal test subjects.

"He called me every day. Two weeks turned to a month. A month to two, and we both missed each other fiercely. He sent me fifty pounds per day from his daily pay every week, so I received the sum of three hundred and fifty pounds every week at the Western Union office. I saved the money in a high-interest savings account. He was happy when I told him how I was saving the money and he told me he was saving at least a hundred pounds daily, too.

*　　*　　*

THE NEWS

In his third month in London, I fell sick. When I did a test at the hospital, I found out I was pregnant.

"I was in total shock. Three months pregnant. Only once in years did I have unprotected sex and it was exactly three months ago with Femi Akinrinola Ajenifuja. It was no surprise that I had become pregnant immediately.

"I was still dazed when I went back to the office to wait for Femi's daily call. When he called, he told me he had concluded his part of the project and would be back in Nigeria after he completed some paperwork the week after. I gathered the courage and told him I was three months pregnant, which I didn't know about as I was still menstruating. That has proven to be a fairly common biological possibility. Neither was there a change in my physical appearance. I didn't even have the normal morning sickness that nearly all pregnant women experienced.

"He screamed from the other end of the phone and I heard the receiver drop as he screamed some more. I was afraid and confused. He came back to the phone and started singing the old hit song by IK Dairo, *'Moso rire o, Eleda mi, mo dupe o.'* He was joyful and couldn't wait to return to his unborn child.

"Smithscon Pharmaceuticals, Nigeria and London gave him a deal of two million pounds up front with a yearly royalty of five thousand pounds. He accepted it and returned to Lagos on the next flight. By evening, he was with me in Jos.

"We lived in Jos for another month before we moved to Abuja and built this beautiful home we live in, here in the heart of Maitama.

"Mummy!" I exclaimed. "I never knew that you and Daddy had such an interesting love story."

"There are many things you do not know, my dear Adeola."

I hugged Mama and stayed in her embrace for quite a while.

My name is Adeola Jemima Ajenifuja and this is my parents' love story.

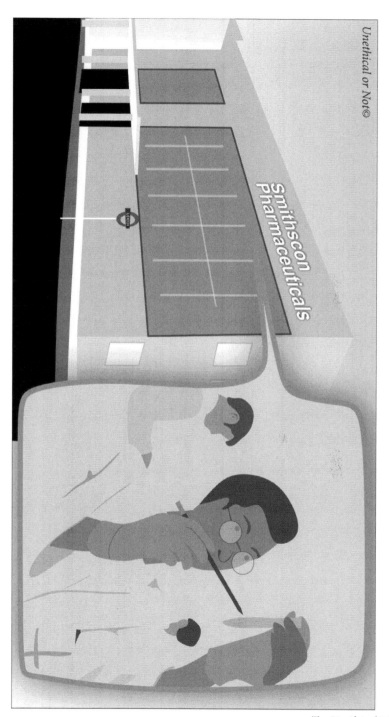

4. Iwalewa & Lade

> " ───────────
> *Success is the result of providence meeting talent*
> *at the right place and time.*"

4. Iwalewa & Lade

"Success is the result of providence meeting talent at the right place and time."

11:00 AM
Friday 24th January, 2020

ARRIVAL

When I arrived at Heathrow Airport, it was quiet, recovering from the rush of the Christmas and New Year holiday season. I delayed my trip until the end of January so that I could get a cheaper flight and avoid the holiday crowd. The British Airways flight from Lagos to London was one of the smoothest I'd ever experienced. Iwalewa was supposed to pick me up but he was engaged at work, so he sent his fiancée Adelade—for short "Lade."

I had not seen Ms. Adelade Tinuke Badejo before. I'd heard so much about her from Iwalewa and had spoken with her on the phone. I had a good idea of what she looked like as her pictures decorated my brother's Facebook and Instagram timelines.

Iwalewa Kodak Ajenifuja had never been so enamoured by a relationship before. He was inebriated by her and didn't complete a sentence without her name falling from his mouth. He constantly quoted funny conversations between them.

Someone called my name in a mellifluous voice. I looked up and saw Lade rushing to welcome me. We shared a hug and connected swimmingly well in no time, like we'd known each other for long.

"Is this your first time in Europe?" she asked, as we headed for the taxi which she booked to take us home.

"I've been to Belgium before. I went for a conference there and spent about a week for a three-day event. I didn't get to see much of the country though."

"Oh! On this trip, you'll get to see as much of the UK as possible. Starting from this ride, we will stop at every place worth seeing and you will see why this is one of the most fantastic places on earth," she said happily. The driver nodded.

We headed for Trafalgar Square and parked on Westminster Street.

"We are close to the Nigerian Embassy," Lade said.

"It's on Northumberland Avenue, Westminster," I mentioned, and she turned and flashed a beautiful smile at me.

"Oh yes!" she said. "Somebody has done her homework already."

We went to Trafalgar Square. The taxi driver helped take several pictures of us. She had booked his taxi for the complete afternoon, so he happily followed us and told us a few historical facts about the city.

"Look at the people moving right in front of us," Lade said pointing at the direction of the moving crowd.

I halted, then faced the direction she was pointing at obediently.

"This is a melting pot of human diversity. People of different colours and shapes—tall; short; average height. All colours from black to brown to white are here. Plump, fat, skinny, tough, mild, broken, fixed, whole, full, satisfied, unsatisfied, satiable, insatiable, angry, sad, beautiful, ugly, attractive or ruddy all find a life here. Isn't it beautiful?" she asked.

"Of course, variety is a spice of life," I answered

We chatted at the backseat of the taxi and proceeded to their home on Oxford Street. Lade informed me that Iwalewa was away at work for three days.

Facebook was rolling out new cookies, including on Instagram and WhatsApp. The cookies sieved valuable data for advertisement purposes, without infringing on subscriber privacy, to prevent replicating a previous data breach scandal with Cambridge Analytica. Because of the scandal, Mark Zuckerberg was summoned for a Congressional hearing. So huge was the scandal that it was deemed instrumental to Donald Trump's election as President of the United States.

Iwalewa worked as head of innovations strategy at the London Office of Facebook. He studied theoretical physics at the University of Ibadan but had built himself up to be multidisciplinary. He had a reasonably strong and reliable insight in every field, with vast knowledge of chemistry, mechanical engineering, energy, world economics, Nigerian and global politics, psychology, marketing and sales, effective communication, quality management systems, innovations development, music, television production, intellectual property rights protection, religion, mental health issues and much more.

His knowledge of each field was as though he had a degree in each discipline. Such was the quality which made him a hot cake for places like Facebook, and other similar corporations that relentlessly tried to poach him. But his first loyalty was to Facebook.

As an innovation strategist for the company, he directed his team on gathering subscriber expectations and desires using high intelligence quotient and ideas decision tree.

Facebook teams were often required to think differently for over 2 billion subscribers, but the 12-man London team focussed on the EU—its laws, data protection policy, etc. Iwalewa's job description was exciting though the job had its toll on the mind. Sometimes it felt like his team were working to save humanity, other times like they were invading public's privacy.

Iwalewa and his fiancée lived in a tastefully furnished apartment decorated with love, and Lade's imprints showed in the glamor and feel of the home. We started making dinner and had small talk.

"How are you guys doing?" I asked.

"We're doing great, Adeola."

"What about you? Anything brewing between you and Chukwuemeka Pahoose? You talked a lot about him in our chats and there are several beautiful pictures of you and him on social media. Any plans?"

"Well, I will tell you about that later when I have settled in," I said to avoid the topic until I left London.

A VENTURE INTO R &D

"Iwalewa tells me you are working on a massive project on Advanced Cryogenic System. Please, tell me more about it," I continued.

"Of course, I am always excited to talk about my work. And I would start from the genesis. Shall we have some food first?" We scooped some food and ate at the dining table.

"Innovations development is a hard nut for everybody," Lade began. "They do not exactly sit us down to run through potential difficulties that lie ahead: the days of eating sardine and bread in the morning, in the afternoon, and for dinner. Then the cycle continues the next day."

"We wish some periods in life never popped up. Journeying through R&D can be one such period."

"That sounds pretty daunting," I said.

Lade chuckled, stretched her hands to the ceiling, and allowed it drop freely to the floor, demonstrating the freefall that could happen in this path.

"You have pushed all your savings into something that is somewhat going to fail. Yet you've got to do it," she continued.

"If you don't push on, you haven't rolled the dice. You haven't even made an attempt. You have not tried your chances to see what fate has in store for you."

She walked to the sofa and beckoned me to join her, as we had finished eating. She then began the story in full.

FLASH OF GENIUS

While my eureka was borne out of a terrible situation, it was a moment of discovery, a flash of genius. It came with the knowledge that even though I could not save the people involved at that time, I had the chance to save some in the future.

"I started my career as a clinical embryologist in 2007 at a budding IVF clinic in Asaba, Nigeria. I got my degree in Microbiology at University of Port Harcourt.

"Our clinic started as an Intra-Uterine Insemination centre. We were into semen preparation and insemination of women with their partners' samples. By 2008, the CEO decided that we should venture into full blown IVF service.

"He acquired IVF standard incubators, an Intracytoplasmic Sperm Injection (ICSI) machine, an inverted microscope and some other equipment. He wanted to acquire cryogenic system for storage of gametes and embryos but at the time he needed four of them. One for storage of semen samples in quarantine. Another for storage of samples already screened. Another for screened oocytes and embryos. And lastly, another as back-up. These cost around two hundred dollars per unit, and the weekly supply of liquid nitrogen was one hundred dollars per week. The cost of the weekly supply was the discouraging factor for him. He could not get a loan or funding anywhere to sustain it and he could not guarantee that he would have enough patients in the first year to maintain the supply.

"Furthermore, the Nigerian government thought that over 180 million people in the country in the 2000s did not need Assisted Reproductive Technology (ART). The will to support such science was absent. The stigmatisation of people who cannot conceive in their bedrooms is a major challenge across African homes, yet the government preferred the orthodox way.

"The government looked away from an opportunity to advance technology. In all fairness, the Nigerian government does not fund technology.

"Thousands of local talents are lying fallow all over the country. Languishing and left untapped. ART is certainly not the only endeavour the government has refused to fund.

"So, my boss sent us to India for a 3-week training on egg

collection, IVF insemination, intracytoplasmic sperm injection, embryo transfer, semen preparation for ICSI and IVF, semen freezing and embryo freezing—the slow freezing. We returned and began our first ICSI and IVF cycles of five patients.

"Four out of the five patients got pregnant. Beginner's luck? We wondered but we were nonetheless excited.

"We did another three cycles after a three-week interval from the first and got 66.7 % success rate. Two out of three women got pregnant in this cycle. We were excited about the success. We had more cycles thereafter, sometimes we got greater success. Other times, things went bad. But what we were doing at the lab began making sense and the business was gaining ground. You can start clapping now," Lade said and chuckled.

I obediently clapped and we both laughed hysterically. Then she continued while we both dug into a bowl of roasted cashewnut.

TURNING POINT

"There is a procedure called Surgical Sperm Retrieval—SSR. We generally apply it to male patients with azoospermia. These are men who lack sperm cells in their ejaculates. Other times, we apply SSR to patients with difficulty producing semen samples on demand.

"It is usually reserved for the urologists who know their way around the testis. In our peculiar Nigerian way, a gynaecologist doubles as a urologist for SSR procedures.

"In the span of one year, we had some success with SSR which was usually planned simultaneously with egg collection. We retrieved sperm cells on the same day of egg collection. The retrieved sperm cells from the testis are injected into eggs via ICSI—one sperm to an egg—and the injected eggs are incubated till day 3 before embryo transfer. Our success with this process only made us bolder. Though we rarely did SSR—about 3 per year—our stats emboldened us.

"Then we had this couple; the man had obstructive azoospermia—he produced sperm but had a blockage preventing it from flowing out with his ejaculate. He underwent tests such as Follicle Stimulating Hormone (FSH) test and Luteinizing Hormone (LH) test. The levels were normal, a subtle indication that there was a high probability that he was producing sperm cells, but there was a roadblock truncating them from meeting with other components of semen in the testes, thereby preventing spermatozoon from flowing out with ejaculate. We therefore planned surgical sperm retrieval alongside egg collection.

"On the day of egg collection, we collected twenty-eight eggs from the woman and, thereafter, performed surgical sperm retrieval on the man. We had a lot of sperm cells retrieved. It was huge.

"We did ICSI and had some leftover retrieved sperm cells which we could have cryopreserved but we had no cryogenic tanks. We had to discard them because there was no means of storage. However, the couple had a number of beautiful embryos for transfer.

"We transferred two embryos and, after two weeks, did a pregnancy test which came out negative. The gynaecologist scheduled the couple for another SSR—egg collection cycle.

"On the scheduled day, we collected thirty-two eggs from the woman. Right after, we did the SSR for the man. We did not find any sperm cell. We searched hard, no single sperm cell.

"The doctor was shocked. 'Just a month ago, we found a lot of sperm. So, what could have happened?' he asked.

"We made ten more attempts. Two trained embryologists checked at a magnification of X20, X40, X100 and 500X. They found nothing. The doctor took more and more tissue from the seminiferous tubules and epididymis. Still we found nothing. He was perplexed. He stepped out of the clinic and stayed away for several hours. I was worried for the young couple because I knew already what the result would be and I feared it.

"Since I was the most senior embryologist on staff, it was my job to deliver the news to the couple.

"The pain, the loss of money and emotional impact of such situation troubled me as I made my way to the couple at the patient waiting room. The nurse had just given the man a painkiller and left.

"I gave them a few minutes to relax while I chatted lightly with them. 'I am sorry, Mr. and Mrs. John Doe, we could not find sperm cells from the surgery, therefore we have to discard the eggs,' I said to them.

"After they calmed down, they wondered if we could store the eggs or preserve them in some way till there was a change in his status. I explained that this eventuality had been explained to them before they signed the consent form. I also reminded them we offered a donor sperm as back up and they refused the option.

"They wondered why we did not have a storage system to store the excess retrieved sperm cells collected from the man a month back, and I told them we had not acquired the technology. They got upset at this and wept in disappointment.

Lade paused and sighed. I held her hands gently.

"Do you think you can still go on with this story?" I asked. She nodded grudgingly.

That was the day I decided to build my own cryogenic system for African labs faced with these limitations," she continued.

"In most societies, distasteful experiences are the drivers of inventiveness."

I began studying the principles of idea development, product development, intellectual property rights protection and Quality Management System (QMS). I decided to apply the knowledge I had gathered on a moderately sized project. I ventured into building a cost-effective data management software for Assisted Reproductive Technology (ART) in Africa.

"The first challenge was hiring the right talent to fill the roles. Software development was not a field I knew anything about. All I had was the idea, so I hired a computer science graduate whom I knew from church to be the intermediary between the software developer and myself to allow me concentrate on the other aspects of running the project.

"Someone from church would seem to have some credibility, right? I had made the perfect choice. Yet the project was jeopardised. There was nothing to show for the money and time we sank into the project. The project was abandoned!

"I didn't give up though. I retried the same project from 2013 through 2017. By this time, an economic recession had hit Nigeria. Companies shut down, IVF clinics closed shop. Even the multinational company Procter and Gamble shut down its $300 million, state-of-the-art production plant in Agbara, Lagos by 2018. It did this just a year after it opened the plant.

"A good product was therefore faced with the debacle of economic crisis.

"The loss broke me. I decided to leave the country for the UK. I applied to study Management at London Business School (LBS). The unprecedented economic crash spurred me to understand business better. So that in future endeavours, I could make better business decisions.

"Business school was smooth; I had the time of my life at LBS, and most of all, it was where I met your brother Iwalewa. He was sent to LBS by Facebook for a short course. I was taking some pictures when he passed in front of my camera, waving.

"I burst into laughter and then he walked towards me. We started talking and it instantly felt as if we had an innate affinity for each other. We found out we were both from Nigeria and he shared interesting stuff about himself. I happily told him things about myself and it was such a pleasure talking with him. We became friends and soon began dating.

"Near the end of my programme at the business school, I got an employment as a clinical embryologist in East London. Iwalewa had just been promoted to Lead Innovations Manager at this time. We moved in together.

"Then I reached out to the UK branch of a Norwegian-owned IVF servicing company concerning my all-time idea for an advanced cryogenic system. I had even christened it *Cryoserve*. At this point, I reminisced about my past failure. It seemed everything in my life was orchestrated to bring me to this point.

"The appointment with the IVF servicing company was on 14th August 2019. Iwalewa had travelled to California three weeks earlier for a scheduled visit to Facebook headquarters in Silicon Valley. Before he left, we prayed fervently about the deal and believed it would pull through.

"It was a big deal, the first time I had gotten close to selling off my intellectual property. This was my major invention!

"There had been several email exchanges and long phone calls over a span of three months prior to the D-Day. The company was a giant conglomerate called *Reproduct*, based in Norway. Its representative from their R&D department flew to the United Kingdom to meet me. The meeting for my presentation was arranged at their office in the outskirts of London.

"I drove my car instead of getting an Uber ride; it was a clean 3.0 engine Jaguar. A beast which drives like it runs on nitrous oxide. It is always a pleasure to sit behind the wheel and listen to the engine purr as it tears up miles on the road.

"The day came but Iwalewa was away. I was confident because he and I had prayed and fasted about it and bound it firm in the name of Jesus. Who knows if my *village people* were watching?

"Anyway, a day before the D-Day, I went to wash my car and had an oil change for the engine. I spent £100 to prepare it solely for that day. Iwalewa and I had just put down all our savings for a purchase of a house and a family car. The month was tough.

"I was going to travel to work and close at 4:30 PM. Then head out for the meeting at a *Reproduct* UK branch at the outskirts of London. The meeting was scheduled for 5:30 PM.

"I got out of my apartment at 7:30 AM, entered my car and started the engine. I drove a few metres and smoke started coming out of the engine. My heart dropped into the bottom of my belly.

"'Today? *Olorun maje o- oh God no*. I reject you in Jesus name!' I muttered under my breath. Iwalewa and I had fasted and prayed, So, that day was supposed to be perfect. God was supposed to hold the day down for me.

"I pulled over and checked what was wrong. The line which supplied water to cool the engine was broken. *What to do?* I thought frantically.

"I found a small piece of cloth at the back of the car and covered the leak. Then I filled the water tank with some water. After driving a few metres, the engine overheated again.

"I was already halfway to work, so I added more water and made it to work thirty minutes late. Immediately I got in, I found some water storage containers and filled them up with water and kept them in the trunk of the car. At the end of the day's work, I was prepared for my meeting with the Norwegian company.

"I could not call the garage to pick up my car because I had exhausted all the allocated funds on the monthly budget for the car for that month in preparing it for the day. Iwalewa was also on a thin budget for the remainder of the month even as he was in America.

"If I dug into the money left, I was *gonna* dig too deep and we hadn't access yet to a bank overdraft since we had lived less than three years in the UK. If I called an Uber, it would have been crazy expensive. In retrospect, I probably had other options I did not see at the time. I eventually risked my damaged car.

"I stopped three times to refill the water. I rushed into the venue at 5:00 PM and I was still 30 minutes early. *Praise the Lord!*

"The representative arrived later for the meeting. I presented my PowerPoint and demonstrated with 3D-printed *Cryoserve* prototype, and he was impressed.

"I gave him the needed materials to present to his company. They would decide to acquire the intellectual property or not.

"We parted ways after an hour of pleasant deliberations. I got back to my car and topped up the water again. It had rained by this time.

"I drove back home and, on entering town, heavy smoke burst out of the car's engine. I parked by the roadside and tried to fan it down. The smoke did not stop, so I waited for two hours for it to fully disperse and for the engine to cool, then I topped it up again.

"I tried to start the car but it wouldn't. I called a garage to pick it up. They reported the engine had knocked. I did not feel bad because my meeting was smooth, and I had faith of beautiful things ahead.

"I sold the damaged car for £180 and got a refund of £560 from the car insurance company. I was at least consoled that the sacrifice was for a greater good.

"The following week, I got an email from the company asking for documents to prove my ownership of the Intellectual Property rights. That was not a problem because I always file for everything around IP rights. I sent all the documents to them. Patent, copyright and trademark registration.

"Few weeks after, I was called for the acquisition process which involved describing the invention in details.

"'*Cryoserve* can be likened to sitting at a Nigerian party, or an *owambe*, as we call it in Nigeria, and getting served with desired food ordered,'" I began explaining.

"'It is very different from a buffet offer, where you stand up and search for what you desire. In getting served at a table by a hostess, you are more relaxed. You are not rummaging through a large crowd of party attendants, standing in a queue to get your food.

"'*Cryoserve* involves getting served medically useful biological materials such as male or female gametes or embryos at a high speed in a typical IVF centre, research centre or biomaterial storage facility. The conventional cryogenic system often requires spending some time locating and bringing out biological materials from a cryogenic system at minus 198 degrees centigrade.

"'*Cryoserve* is engineered to sort biological materials faster and safer once you punch the three-digit code allocated as the ID for each unique sample.

"'In addition to the speed and ease of sample storage and retrieval, *Cryoserve* produces its own liquid nitrogen (fuel for Cryogenic system). *Cryoserve* does this via advanced fractional distillation of atmospheric air using a patented Distiller cum Mega-Gas processor capable of processing 1,000 litres of atmospheric air per hour.'"

"I ran through the 3-D design and explained the physics and engineering behind *Cryoserve* to the company. Its chief engineer, Engr. Anthony Piotrowski, asked various questions and I answered them brilliantly. I was asked to leave the room for ten minutes and was invited back in after seven minutes."

"'Ms. Lade Tinuke Badejo, we are highly impressed by your presentation. First things first, what do you want to do? Sell or scale up *Cryoserve* with us?'" Engr. Piotrowski asked.
"I responded, 'I want to sell it

"'For your work and the transfer of the entire intellectual property of *Cryoserve*, we are willing to offer you a sum of £400,000,'" the CEO, Dr. Louise Macintosh, said.

"I loved the offer, but I knew I could get more. After all, I had learned negotiation during my days at the London Business School.

"I asked for £600,000 and gave them beautiful reasons why *Cryoserve* was even worth more. We settled at £550,000.

Before I signed the contract, I asked for two favours. One, that they retain the name *Cryoserve*; and two, that they sell to African labs at a highly discounted rate.

"They obliged easily. That was how *Cryoserve* was acquired for more than half a million Great Britain pounds. I was credited the same day after signing all the relevant acquisition papers. My life and Iwalewa's changed in that instant.

"When your ambition is tethered to persistence, success and reward will eventually find you at the end of the tunnel."

"Iwalewa and I are looking at starting our own company with the money. We hope his severance package, when he leaves Facebook, can be added to my *Cryoserve* sale returns.
"We are considering starting an innovations development company with branches in Nigeria and Kenya, the headquarters in London. Iwalewa considers leaving his job at Facebook by the middle of this year. We hope our plan goes as desired."

"Wao, the heavens have been fair to you guys," I said, after an exciting listening pleasure. When I noticed that she had regained her composure, I said to her: "I hope the universe breathes into your plans and makes everything to fall in place for you."

It was already 3:14 AM. We had been sitting in the living room for hours while she told me this story of an amazing journey in the world of innovations. I told her I needed to rest; we would do more talking the next day.

Lade's story redefined ambition for me.

She had taken two weeks off work to spend time with me. We had plans and scheduled activities for my stay in London. This was my first time in the UK, and I was going to paint the town red. I also hoped to see the Queen and get a handshake from Her Majesty.

My name is Adeola and this is Iwalewa and Adelade's R & D story.

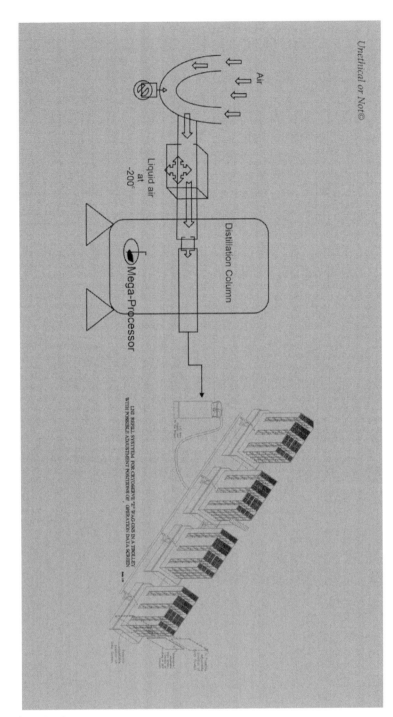

Air

Liquid air at -200°

Distillation Column

Mega-Processor

LNG REFILL SYSTEM FOR CRYOSERVE "T" WAGON IN A TROLLEY WITH POSSIBLE ADJUSTMENT POSITION OF OPERATION DATA SCREEN

5. In the time of covid

Days roll into weeks, weeks into months, and months into years, yet time is an uncanny package full of woes and beautiful surprises."

5. In the Time of Covid

"Days roll into weeks, weeks into months, and months into years, yet time is an uncanny package full of woes and beautiful surprises."

February, 2020

PAINTING THE TOWN RED

My first week at Iwalewa's was electrifying. Lade and I had a brief tourist moment at The British Museum in London and at another museum at Liverpool. We marvelled at different artifacts taken from West Africa in the African section of both museums. We saw various priced collectors' items from other continents as well.

At the docks of the Liverpool museum, there were lots of stories and memorabilia about transatlantic slavery and artifacts to go with them. The museum's grotesque details couldn't escape our eyes; such inhumane recollection of history perplexed and saddened us. Though it wasn't Lade's first time there, the pallor on her face expressed renewed horror.

After the museums, we visited Manchester and Leeds, before returning to London in the second week because Lade had to resume work that week. Iwalewa also took time off work after a nonstop marathon stay at his office. He was pumped to show me around as well.

During my second week, Iwalewa and I decided to visit other European countries. We planned to have a good time touring those countries. Then, the world came to its first-phase rehearsal of the coronavirus in faraway Wuhan, China. Christened "COVID-19" to denote Corona-Virus-Disease-Of-2019, the virus soon started claiming lives.

Iwalewa and I only spent a few hours in Amsterdam when news of lockdown reached us, and we quickly returned to the UK on the next flight. At home, we buckled under government-imposed restriction on movement and business.

It was the most unbelievable time in history. Even almighty United States of America, always in the forefront of things, capitulated under the strong arm of the pandemic. TV shows like *ER, 911, Grey's Anatomy, Amsterdam, Code Black, House*

MD, The Good Doctor, The Resident etc., depicted America as the bastion of medicine, but the pandemic debunked that.

Then came the conspiracy theories. The virus was caused by the 5G network, some claimed. Something about emission of radioactive waves. In Africa, the pandemic inspired interesting political incidents. The President of Uganda attempted to postpone presidential election in his country by four years. Back home in Nigeria, government's response to the health crisis was as embarrassing as the president's inability to pronounce "Covid-19," which he called Covik One-Nine.

PONTUS PILATE OF LAGOS

In Lagos, the governor was nicknamed Pontus Pilate of Lagos for his notorious showmanship at cooked up projects and activities pretending to check the pandemic. On 11th February 2020, Pontus Pilate of Lagos banned the use of motorcycles and *keke* on all Lagos roads. The worst-hit by the *okada* and *keke* ban were companies like Gokada, OPay and Max.ng, which had poured over $250 million into the state's bike-hailing economy. Earlier, they had been licensed to operate by the same government that later banned them. The streets, therefore, were filled with jobless youths and stranded commuters alike. Somehow rumour spread that the ban meant to hand a monopoly to a cab-hailing company owned by the governor's cousin.

I called home to speak with my parents. My mother had become diabetic, I learnt after the call. I was worried for the timing of her diagnosis. Hospitals were already overwhelmed in the UK. I wondered what the situation was in Nigeria. I called Iwalewa to join the conversation. Lade, too, joined us, alarmed by the news.

"Has a second opinion been sought?" I asked. My father said, yes.

My mother said indeed, a specialist friend confirmed the diagnosis. We had a conference call with her doctor friend who gave second opinion to confirm the diagnosis.

Interestingly, I knew the doctor-Dr. Babatunde Ogunkile, who grew up as friends with my mother in Omu-Aran. He now worked in Abuja Diabetics Centre, Kubwa. Apart from taking insulin injections, Dr. Ogunkile advised, my mother should switch to using unripe plantain instead of yam to make pounded yam-to help manage her sugar level.

"I now have my own pot," my mother said to me.

"Is that so?" I asked.

"And I now have to eat a lot of vegetables or food with a lot of fibre. Plus, I don't use regular salt anymore."

The salt, composed of *Variant* Natrium Chloride (*v*NaCL), has almost no impact on blood pressure and is suitable for diabetic patients who have risks of high-blood pressure. It was invented by a chemistry student from a novel R&D university in Abuja.

I had always thought the biochemistry of using unripe plantain was due to the presence of trioses, a group of monosaccharide carbohydrates bearing 3-carbon instead of the traditional 6-carbon sugar. Therefore, the glycolysis pathway is circumvented. But to my surprise, my knowledge of this pathway diverged far from the point. Dr. Ogunkile gave me a copious explanation of the principle behind the prescription of unripe plantain to diabetic patients.

Gesticulating as he spoke on Zoom video call, he said the slow and steady release of glucose in unripe plantain helps in diabetics management.

"Generally, when the body has received excess glucose in the liver and is unable to use it, it converts the excess glucose to glycogen via insulin produced by the pancreas in the liver. In the event of abnormality in the pancreas leading to diabetes, excess glucose is not stored as should be and this results in elevated blood glucose. In the long run, complications such as high blood pressure and organ failures emerge. So, it's better to eat food that would digest and release glucose into the blood slowly.

"Simple sugars digest faster than complex sugars. Hence, it is generally advised that diabetics consume complex sugars to ensure that glucose is released into the blood at a slower rate. Also, meals that are high in fibre are advised. Unripe plantain contains more complex carbohydrates; thus, it takes longer to digest, releasing glucose to the blood slowly. Also, it is high in fibre and vitamins," he said.

His hospital was filling up with politicians infected with COVID-19, so he had little time to be with us and soon asked to log out of the conference call.

"I hope you are observing COVID-19 measures and closely following the diabetes management?" I asked my parents. To both they answered yes. From then, we kept a tab on them to ensure all was well.

Soon after, the virus began plaguing countries. The United Kingdom also started recording deaths, with the United States topping the leaderboard of coronavirus deaths. Its president, Donald J. Trump, was negligent about the virus which he called the Chinese virus. But the virus came deadly upon his country like a thief in the night. Italy was already hard-hit by this time, with bodies dropping everywhere and suicide rates spiking. Fatality rose to over a million worldwide.

Countries built new facilities and hospitals to match the threat of the virus.

Nigeria played ping-pong with the pandemic but not for long; COVID-19 took the life of the president's Chief of Staff - Abba Kyari. Soon after, it took the life of a corrupt former governor of Oyo State, Senator Ajimobi.

Political rallies still held in some parts of the country, especially in Oyo State, where the sitting governor Ayo Makinde carelessly approved his party's unconscionable request for a rally.

"Nigeria is a crime scene; she is a pandemic away from absolute extinction."

HASHTAG #BLM

My stay in the UK was supposed to be short, even though I had a two-year multiple visa. I planned to stay for a month as I had several activities lined up in Nigeria. By May, countries began lifting the lockdown, but just then the world was shaken by the murder of George Floyd, an unarmed Black man, by a Minneapolis police officer. Floyd's harrowing death was captured on video, showing the officer kneeling on his neck for over eight minutes while another officer barred people from interrupting the grotesque spectacle. Two other officers held him down, literally abetting the murder in plain sight. His death changed so many things and was like an answer to the prayer for a Black Jesus.

For the first time, coloured people became more visible (apologies to Ralph Ellison). In the United Kingdom, John Boyega, a British actor of Nigerian descent led a massive *Black Lives Matter* demonstration in London. I was there. In Palestine, a mural of George Floyd was painted on a spot at West Bank, a point of separation between Israel and Palestine. There were murals in Muslim countries like Afghanistan and Pakistan painted in the capital cities of Kabul and Karachi respectively. In Ireland, Belgium, Amsterdam, Italy and France, there were also Black Lives Matter protests. It was a global outrage.

While Mr. George Floyd was dying, he begged to see his mother; then said, "I can't breathe," which became the slogan for the protests worldwide. "I Can't Breathe" was inscribed on face masks worn by many protesters. An outraged, white US Marine veteran, Todd Winn, staged a one-man Black Lives Matter protest under 99°F Utah heat for three hours. His face mask bore "I Can't Breathe," too. In Nigeria, the renowned Smithscon Pharmaceuticals changed her name to *Carbon Floyd Pharmaceuticals* in support of the Floyd's death protests. Sadly, many more Black lives were taken in USA even after the uproar about Mr. Floyd's death.

My stay in the UK was prolonged as a result of the pandemic. Flights out of the country did not begin till late July 2020. I was finally able to return to Nigeria late September 2020 as Nigerian international airports did not reopen until that time. I came back to rejoin my family and friends in Nigeria and was glad to meet them all in good health; not a soul was infected with COVID-19.

My name is Adeola Jemima Ajenifuja and this is my story.

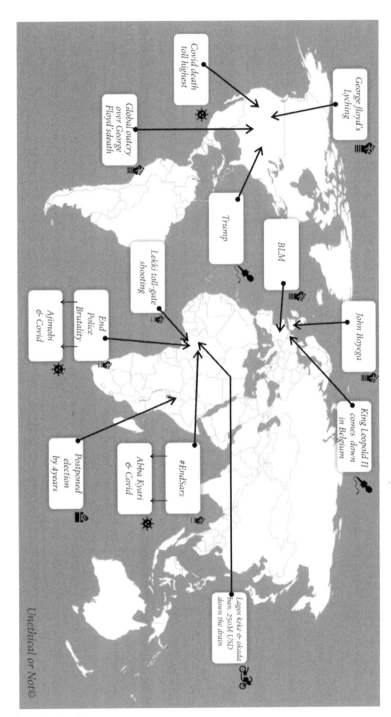

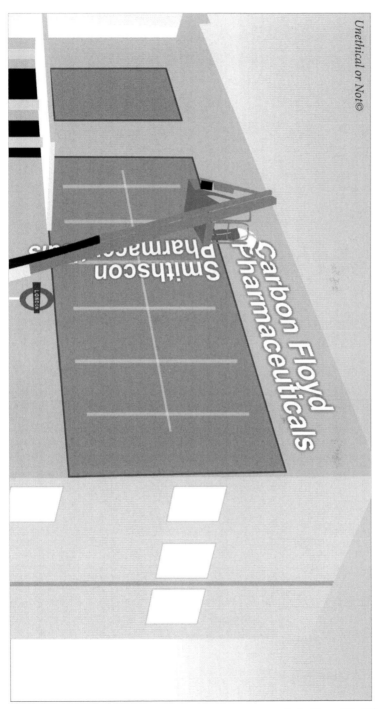

6. Unexpected turn of events

> " ———————————————
> *A set date is not set until the day has fully unfolded.*"

6. Unexpected Turn of Events

"A set date is not set until the day has fully unfolded."

8:30 AM
Wednesday 26th February, 2025

ADRENALINE PUMPING

A bullet struck the side door of the Mercedes-Benz car ahead of us, shattered the window glass and snapped the neck of the occupant in the front passenger seat. It happened in milliseconds. More bullets flooded the car. Iwalewa impulsively reversed ours and shouted, "Everybody, go down low." I was in the car, with my parents and Jumoke.

The beleaguered car tried to reverse from the entrance of the courthouse but failed. I took a second peek at it and saw that even more shots were fired without any consideration for its occupants. The bullets shattered its windshields, and it didn't seem like anyone could escape such multiple shots launched at a single target.

The shots came from the direction of Savannah Municipal Bank, which bordered Abuja Municipal Court where hearing for my case held. It was a robbery and a group of policemen engaged the robbers in a fusillade from an adjacent building in whose crossfire the car ahead of us was trapped, the attack endangering my whole family.

Iwalewa's deftness in such precarious situation must have come from his briefly attending the Kaduna Military Secondary School. He drove us out of danger like a professional. I stopped him about a kilometre from the gunfire.

"Stop the car! Please, stop the car," I shouted.

"Why are we stopping?" he countered and decelerated reluctantly.

"I hope we are not going back? Being a medical doctor does not confer automatic superpower," he said.

"No, we are not going back. I am," I said.

"Why do you want to go back to a danger zone? What good will it do anyone to leap into a valley of death?" my mother asked.

"I'm a doctor and that place is going to need rapid response from what we just saw. I'm needed," I answered.

"But you are not a specialist in trauma medicine. You are pretty much a *pregnant* gynaecologist; you will pose more risk than offer any help in such adrenaline-pumping arena," my father added.

"Well, I could handle a few issues that require basic medicine and I can do it some reasonable distance away from the danger."

Jumoke said she'd go with me to caution me and offer assistance to the victims of the shootings.

"A pregnant gynaecologist and a plastic surgeon rushing to save lives, would that not be a sight?" my father asked sarcastically.

We picked a first aid box from the boot of the car and left.

Iwalewa went on with my parents. Jumoke and I watched them drive off; then we trekked a little until we saw an ambulance come towards us. We stopped it and introduced ourselves as medical doctors, flashing our individual IDs-mine for Abuja Municipal Hospital where I worked, and Jumoke's, from Teflon Plast Medical Centre, Liverpool.

The team on the ambulance were glad to have us. Their leader, Dr. Opeoluwa Adewumi, a Unilorin-trained trauma surgeon, mentioned that she once worked in Afghanistan with the United Nations. She looked so skinny I did not think she could survive much pressure.

"She would break," I mumbled, carelessly.

She gave me a quick glance and said, "I get that all the time."

I was about to explain myself when she interposed- "I assume you are familiar with a crash cart?" She pointed at the crash cart which contained all the medications and other aids we needed to handle an emergency.

"Yes, we are," Jumoke and I chorused. I couldn't resist the urge to roll my eyes. How could a doctor not be familiar with a crash cart?

"Hand me those mini defibrillators and prepare the black bags, Dr. Tee," she said, and the lady she earlier introduced as Dr. Omidan Tiwátópé quickly handed her the defibrillators.

"Put one in each bag and give to everyone. We are a 5-man team with Drs. Adeola and Jumoke who have been given the privilege to work with us today."

"Dr. Ajenifuja, I hope you will be fine in the field with your pregnancy? I naturally would not have given you privilege but we need as much hands as we can get. If you feel any discomfort, please, inform me," Dr. Adewumi said.

I nodded.

"We are here!" the driver said.

We camped at a safe distance from the Abuja Municipal Court and Savannah Municipal Bank. Dr. Adewumi spoke on a radio with the coordinating police officer on site, who said four of his men and two civilians were wounded and would be brought to us.

In two minutes, they arrived on stretchers. We shared the wounded persons to our numbers. I checked the pulse of one gunshot victim; it was weak. I tore off the fabric from the gunshot area to have a better visual and then checked if there was an exit wound. The wound was on the left side of his chest. The bullet only grazed him. I reached for a sterile gauze and cleaned the wounds and bandaged him up. He began to open his eyes and his pulse got better. He must have been in shock, otherwise he should not have been brought to us.

Jumoke's patient was dead. A policewoman. She was already dead before she was brought to us.

Dr. Adewumi relieved Jumoke of the dead policewoman and asked her to attend to a young boy who was just brought to us, herself reviving a patient and checking his vitals one more time. She asked the driver to bring in more gauze from the crash cart and asked Omidan how her patient fared.

"My patient has been patched up. There was an exit wound, but I was able to stop the bleeding," Omidan replied.

My second patient had a bullet lodged in his left leg. I gave him 30mls of pentazocine, snapped a new pair of gloves on and reached for the bullet. I checked if there was any other gunshot wound. There wasn't.

Just then, more ambulances arrived. The police had subdued the armed robbers and arrested five of them, two shot dead.

Jumoke's second patient survived and was bandaged up. I went ahead and checked the occupants of the car earlier caught in the crossfire. None of them had a pulse; they were all dead. There was no rescue attempt during the shooting due to the crossfire.

Omidan received a second patient, an elderly woman with no noticeable wound but shut eyes. She checked if the woman was breathing and connected her to medical grade oxygen supply. The woman regained consciousness some minutes after.

Dr. Adewunmi received one more officer who was already dead. I received a phone call from my mother and told her we were okay. I heard joyful murmurs from all of them and I smiled for the first time since the incident began. The bodies of the family in the car were removed. A book fell from the car and I picked it up. An inscription on the first page read: "To my son Folorunso Olasegiri in whom I am well pleased." A dam of poignant emotions in me threatened to break. Tears slid gently from my eyes.

I strolled to the court to find out if the tragic incident affected my case. The clerk said all cases scheduled for that day had been moved forward till Tuesday next week.

*   *   *

LIVES AND PROPERTY

It was the sixth day since the shooting. I walked past the TV in our living room when I saw President, Are-Ona Kankan-Afo set to deliver a speech. Maybe he would speak about the deaths from the robbery. So, I stood to watch.

"Today, I present myself to you as a failure-an unworthy leader whose shot at a target missed and claimed seven valuable lives. That should never have happened on Nigerian soil.

"Our crime rate in the Republic has reached an unprecedented level since I took office. My efforts to work with the Senate and use Artificial Intelligence to improve security, safety, and protect lives and property have ended in a stalemate, misrepresented as a campaign for invading the privacy of Nigerians.

"I have therefore filed a lawsuit following constitutional provisions to bypass the Senate's unfavourable blockage of a measure that can save Nigerian lives.

"Five civilians lost their lives in that robbery incident in Abuja. One of them was Folorunso Olasegiri, 13-year-old son of Folakemi Olasegiri and Ayoola Olasegiri, who equally died in the attack. The couple also lost their daughter Arotile Tolulope Olasegiri, a scientist working on a cost-effective way to source alternative energy from cassava crops. Their friend who was with them in the car, Aderopo Bolutife, was a tech engineer who just raised venture capital to build an app that would help Nigerians share and create innovative ideas. These were real people. Innocent Nigerians with hopes and aspirations, only without the security enjoyed by members of the Senate.

"Two police officers Sergeant Toni Okoro and D.P.O Effiong Kokoma were killed in the attack. I spoke to their families the other day and the pain still haunts me. It should haunt every politician who, through rhetoric or silence, has undermined the proposal to deploy technology to keep Nigerians safe.

"During my campaign, I made it known that securing Nigerian lives would be a priority in my presidency, that the safety of lives and the protection of property would be close to my heart. It is heartbreaking that this promise lies largely unfulfilled.

"We have succeeded in realising most of our campaign promises. We have delivered advanced and affordable healthcare across the country. We have bettered our power supply-Nigerians now enjoy a twenty-hour power supply every day. We have improved the economy. The naira is now a hundred to a dollar.

"We have given the minority and other marginalised groups more strategic positions in the running of the country. Errors of our past leaders which led us to a Civil War have been corrected with reparations and equitable governance. Conditions have improved for our citizens, but they have to stay alive to enjoy them. They waited this long and played their part in building a nation, and the security to reap from their own labor is a primary function of government. In this, we failed them.

"Today, our failure to protect Master Folorunso Dare Olasegiri, Mrs. Folakemi Asake Olasegiri, Mr. Ayoola Daniel Olasegiri, Ms. Arotile Tolulope Olasegiri, Ms. Aderopo Opo Bolutife, Officer Toni Kan Okoro, and D.P.O Effiong Adam Kokoma has dented our stellar record.
"We failed these seven beautiful souls.

"However, my promise remains. Nothing like this will ever happen again. I have received confirmation from my Chief of Staff that the Supreme Court has approved the implementation of AI's predictive technologies in fighting crime. This system has ninety-eight per cent accuracy. And it shall, in no way, breach any privacy laws.

"I mourn these deaths and once more apologise to the bereaved families for government's failure to secure all of us. But I believe that henceforth we are in a good position to hope for a better tomorrow. God bless Nigeria. God bless the people's Republic of Nigeria."

A spell of silence remained after the president ended his speech-no one watching it moved for several seconds. When we recovered from the momentary silence, we exited the house. We lined up and looked at father's black bulletproof hummer jeep, like Dominic Toretto and his crew after they lost Paul Walker in *Fast & Furious*.

COURT REOPENS

Last week's crossfire and the loss of innocent lives still shook us six days later.

About a year ago, a black bulletproof jeep was gifted to my father as part of his yearly royalty for the patent of Olamol. The company wanted to keep him safe. Amazing how much value these White men placed on a human life special to them. My father, however, rarely drove it as he deemed it too ostentatious. He did not like attention.

As we walked to the jeep to go for the rescheduled hearing of my case, we heard a buzz at the gate. My father checked the intercom app on his phone to see who it was. The visitor was not visible, and network affected the audio. I told them to stay in the car while I checked who was at the gate.

"Why are you here, Ada?" I asked as I opened the small gate.

She said she heard about the shooting on the news and came to check if my family was alright.

Ada was my father's young friend. She studied Botany at University of Maiduguri. I don't know how they met, but the minute she knew my father was a big name in drug discovery in Africa and that he even owned a drug patent, she drew close to him and the family.

I never trusted her much. The smiles and laughter when she visited were suspicious. I always sensed a hidden plan beneath the mentorship she claimed to seek from my father.

My father was rich after all and it was easy to see why an intelligent, beautiful twenty-four-year-old graduate of Botany, with specialisation in the application of *eleusine indica* in the treatment of hypertension, suddenly developed a strong interest in him. My father often enjoyed her company and sang her praises. The chemistry between them might have been based on a love for science and invention, but wasn't that how Pierre Curie behaved with Marie, another woman, while discovering Radium, leaving his wife in penury and never looking back?

My mother trusted my father though; she believed the relationship was purely academic, an affair of science. My mother studied secretarial studies, so sometimes when my father chatted with Ada, I understood the desire he filled up.

I told Ada the family was fine and had an event; she could come another time. Besides, she already knew we did not die in the shooting. She looked dejected as she left, and I felt bad.

Iwalewa drove the jeep out of the compound and we headed towards Abuja Municipal Court. Jumoke and my parents sat at the back, Iwalewa and I at the front.

Our arrival at the court was emotional, filled with anxiety. Six days ago, we almost became penumbras of life. I didn't think I would be able to call my witnesses for the day, but I summoned courage. We all got out of the car.

My counsel was already waiting, and we took our seats in the courtroom. Judge Amaradi was present. LP Gida and the Pahoose family were already seated. The jury walked in and took their seats and the court session began.

I called Mrs. Chinyere Pahoose to the witness stand and cross-examined her.

"Good morning, Mrs. Pahoose. I just have a few questions about your son Engr. Chukwuemeka Pahoose."

She looked scornfully at me but remained calm.

"Ask your questions, 'Deola," she said in a calm tone.

"When last did you and your husband see your son before he died? Please, remember you are under oath, ma. It will be highly appreciated if you take your time to recall," I said in an equally calm manner.

After thinking for a few seconds, she unwillingly said, "Five years before he died."

The building stirred. Judge Amaradi gavelled at least five times to calm the court down.

I paused while we all calmed down, then I asked another question.

"Within those five years you didn't see him, did you ever speak with your son?"

"No," she said.

"Not even once?" I asked with my eyes firmly on the jury bench.

"Not even once," she snapped.

"So, you do not know if your son had a testament or a will in case of his death?"

The jury now became more interested and concentrated even more.

"My son was a very young healthy man. He was full of life. How could someone barely 30 years old have a will?"

"Actually, your son was 29 years old before his unfortunate death."

"I am an old woman; you can't expect my memory to be sound like yours. Either way, my son was too young to keep a will," she said imperiously.

"Mrs. Pahoose, this is 2025. People write wills as early as possible now, ma," I said. "He and I made several attempts to patch things up with you and his father but for some reasons you were unwilling to let go."

"Objection, my Lord, counsel is testifying," Gida interrupted abruptly.

"Withdrawn!" I responded and proceeded to ask my next question.

"Do you even know what he did? Do you? He disrespected us, you made him disrespect us," she argued.

"No, I do not, Madam Pahoose. All I can recall was, you and Daddy Pahoose did not provide money to process his admission and I had that money and gave him. I only helped him because he was my friend-

"-Objection, Your Honour," Gida interjected. "Counsel is assassinating my client's dignity through unrelated concerns."

But Mrs. Pahoose screamed at me before the Judge could comment, "What effrontery! 'Deola, in our family, we do everything by ourselves, we do not take handouts and my son should have forfeited that admission and waited for another time."

"I'm sorry, Dr Ajenifuja, you shan't continue questioning Mrs. Pahoose with such concerns."

"Apologies, Your Honour," I said and adjusted the hem of my dress.

"Move it along Dr. Ajenifuja and get to the point," Judge Amaradi said.

Mrs. Pahoose burst into tears and I handed her a tissue.

I walked to LP Gida and handed him an exhibit.

"This is exhibit B10, Your Honour," I said as I handed a copy of the document to the clerk who in turn gave it to the Judge. I also gave Mrs. Pahoose a copy to read to the court.

"Mrs. Pahoose, please, can you take a look at this document? That's your son's will and final testament, and it indicates there that if anything happened to him, Adeola Jemima Ajenifuja-that is me-was allowed to decide what to do with his belongings and, if a medical issue, I was to choose for him."

She answered tearfully, "That does not give you the right to desecrate his corpse."

"I would never disrespect my best friend like that. I did what I had to, to help continue his life in some way. He went through so much and his life was taken abruptly. So, I wanted his life to be propagated in some way. I did not want him to end just like that.

"I have no further question for this witness, Your Honour," I said and walked to my seat.

Mr. Gida had no questions for Mrs. Pahoose either.

The Judge adjourned the case and scheduled the last witness for the week after.

*   *   *

THE DEPARTED

"Hope is not a promise of fulfillment at the end of the rope. It is not a vehicle of certainty. It is merely a passage that leads to utopia or complete nothingness. Yet, hope is good. Hope is needful. It is like a natural antidepressant, while we tarry for the things to come, the things that can make or mar us."

I read the words above from the book I took off Folorunso Olasegiri's body and I remembered them now as we stood together in mourning. The book was supposed to be packaged as an evidence along with other personal effects. I felt drawn to that family for no particular reason, most especially to their son Folorunso Olasegiri.

We were at a graveyard in Gwagwalada, Abuja, to bury victims who died from the shootings. Everyone was present. Jumoke, Ada, Mumsie, Iwalewa, Daddy, Dr. Omidan Tiwátópé and Dr. Opeoluwa Adewumi, all dressed in black. We came to pay our respects to both the deceased policemen and the Olasegiri family. The place was congested and swarmed by journalists.

A strange number called my phone; its country code was +324, which is the country code for Belgium. The only person I knew in Belgium was Wito Broekaert. Oh yes! I knew someone else there too whom Wito introduced to me: his beautiful friend Margot. I did not recognise the number. It was possible that it could be either of them.

I picked the call on the last ring and it was indeed Wito as suspected. He had heard about what happened in the news, too.

I met Wito during my one-week visit to Belgium for a 3-day event. I attended the Belgian Society for Assisted Reproductive Technology (BSART) conference that year in 2019, long before *Chuks* passed. I had read on Wikipedia that Intracytoplasmic Sperm Injection was invented in Belgium, so I decided to attend the conference to get a feel. Shockingly, I was the only Black person at the conference, and it felt uncomfortable.

Wito appeared from nowhere and introduced himself. I was surprised he spoke English. Not exactly surprised though, now that I think about it carefully. The conference had people from England, Germany, Holland, and, of course, me from

Nigeria, and it was conducted in English.

Well, Wito struck up a conversation. I was impressed that he knew Africans do not walk around with lions. He was broadminded and widely read. He knew things about other African countries I did not even know. He worked for an IVF servicing company in the outskirts of Brussels, which was a major donor and sponsor of the conference.

After my first day, I returned to my lodging, a first-class, famous hotel in Noordstation, Brussels. Wito came in the evening with his friend Margot Luyckfasseel. They came to take me out. He did a quick introduction and Margot and I hit it off immediately.

We went shopping. At a point, Wito gave us girls some space to talk. Margot had a special brand of jeans styling unique to her, so we went into the shops and she told me to try them on. I did and I loved them. She offered to pay but I refused.

I paid for the pair of jeans. We bought make-up boxes, chocolates and all. We eventually went to get some Belgian beer. OMG, Belgian beer is the best. It reminded me of palm wine back home. There is a particular order for beer called *een pint*, as in "one pint," from the beer tap. It was the same measurement we use in the hospital when we say, "One pint of blood."

We eventually went on to Wito's apartment, where Margot also had a room. It was in Molenbeek-the popular Bruxelles, Molenbeek. Wito's apartment was a loft. Other occupants of the loft came also and Wito introduced me to them. They all pecked me on both cheeks, 2 x 13 pecks on a single night. We had a swell time and I took an Uber back to my hotel at 2:00 AM.

All through my stay in Belgium, I spent the evenings with Wito and Margot and always left late. We had an amazing time and took so many pictures.

"Are you alright? I heard about the attacks in Abuja. I just called to know if you were not involved," he said compassionately into the phone when I picked up.

"I am fine. Thank you for calling. I was near the crossfire with my family, but we are safe."

He passed the phone to Margot and we spoke at length as women tend to do and I told her about the current happenings in my life.

Before we said goodbyes, I invited them for the dedication of my baby. "It will be in four months." They agreed they would be in Nigeria by then. I was pleased to hear that. I reluctantly told them I had to get off the phone to observe the funeral. After a round of goodbyes, we hung up.

The funeral arrangement was made for a single pastor to preside over. Soon the bodies were laid to rest.

My name is Adeola Jemima Ajenifuja and this is my story.

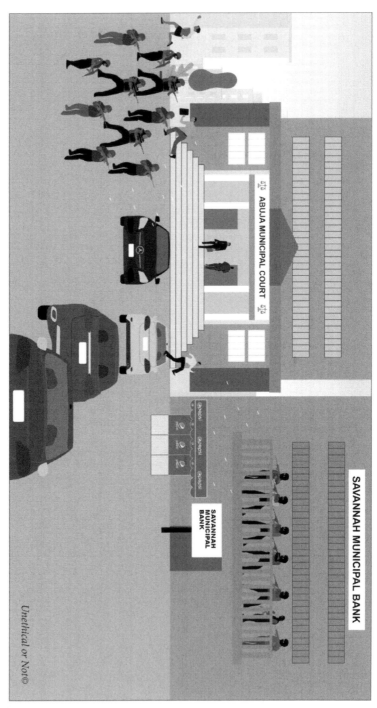

7. The Birth of an Enigma

" ─────────────────────────

A dig is often satisfying, whether it is purposed to

unveil a fossil or to find oneself."

7. The Birth of an Enigma

"A dig is often satisfying, whether it is purposed to unveil a fossil or to find oneself."

8:00 AM
Monday 1st December, 1997

I must have cringed in discomfort inside my mama's uterus as the driver's foot slammed the breaks and suddenly halted the car. Grandma Feyisayo unfastened her seatbelt, flung the car door open and sprang out, shouting incoherently.

The driver jumped out too with great haste, with my grandma's neighbour Baba Dimeji. The two men disappeared into the private hospital of the Evangelical Church of West Africa (ECWA) at Egbe-a part of old Kwara State now in Kogi-to the emergency room, shouting on top of their voices. They had driven several hours from Omu-Aran to this recommended hospital.

They came back seconds later pushing a stretcher with the help of a nurse who joined them. My grandma and Baba Dimeji helped Mama out of the car and carefully laid her on the stretcher and headed for the labour room.

A Caucasian, middle-aged doctor joined us at the entrance of the hospital; he started checking Mama's vitals. She seemed to be in agony-her beautiful face looked pale and contorted from labour pains.

"Madam, what is your name?" the doctor asked, scribbling down details.
"Oludayo." Her words were faint and showed that, in uttering those syllables, she was atrophying.
"Sorry?" the young doctor asked.
"Oludayo ... Oludayo Yusuf is my name. Is my baby safe?"
"I will inform you as soon as I am sure, Oludayo," the doctor responded, hanging the stethoscope back on his neck.
"Who is the father of the child?" he asked looking in Baba Dimeji's direction.
"Who is he?" the doctor asked a second time.
"Baba Dimeji is family but not the father," Grandma responded.

Grandma moved closer to the doctor and said, "The father is on his way from Lagos, the big city."

Soon after, Grandma and Baba Dimeji discussed my mama's condition and options with the doctor in charge and the rest of the medical team. A gentle nurse, Lola Thorpe, attended to Mama.

The medical team had some update, but the news they bore about me was not a good one.

"It looks like we will have to conduct an immediate caesarean section," the doctor said. "Oludayo has a narrow pelvis, which has resulted in the protracted labour."

"What is a narrow pelvis? Is it a kind of sickness?" Grandma Feyisayo asked, genuinely confused.

"A narrow pelvis results in difficult natural-push delivery. An operation is often required," the doctor explained carefully to an apprehensive Grandma.

Just then, Mama made a loud noise clutching her belly which bulged a little stronger like a well-oiled gourd. The doctor rushed to her side to calm her, then she asked a question that made me giggle.

"Doctor, is it possible to vomit a baby? Because right now, I feel as if my baby is moving upwards to my throat, and I am feeling nauseous too."

"No, no… madam you cannot vomit a baby. It is impossible," he replied, stifling a laugh through his thin lips.

The doctor later discovered that I was fighting for survival since I realized that I could not be birthed normally. I had moved upwards to avoid drowning in the amniotic fluid, and up was my only hiding place.

Maybe it was genetics or epigenetic adaptation, or, perhaps survival instinct. It remains a phantom to me, how a T-minus two hours old infant possessed such wisdom. How did I know that I had to do something to survive? That to live I had to swim upward?

"A fetus wanted to live, it avoided drowning by swimming up, a trait shared with adults who spring from rock bottom to the top when there is nowhere else to go."

*   *   *

INNATE SURVIVAL SKILLS

I wanted to see the world, I wanted to have my share in the world's struggles, victories, pains, pleasures, and whatever fate would cast my path. I was undoubtedly anxious.

How I conceived to use my tiny brain cells then still surprises me. I know they were not exactly fully formed, but those few cells were useful for survival that day. It was a primal epiphany to my tiny body-the innate instinct for survival encoded in every cell, every organism, regardless of its size.

Could this be the reason, during an intracytoplasmic sperm injection (ICSI), sperm cells do rapid accelerations from the touch of an ICSI pipette? Even gametes possibly have some sort of brain, maybe microscopic, but there must be a neural effect that reminds them to stay out of danger and survive. Like the sperm cell, I wanted to live.

"Ma, we are shadows on the wall of time," the young Caucasian doctor said tenderly to my family. He gave consent forms to Grandma. "These documents are required to be signed before we can proceed with the surgery. We want to do everything within our power to save mother and child as quickly as possible."

"No, doctor. I am not going to consent to an operation that can lead to the death of my grandchild, or worse, the mother. No way," Grandma cried in despair.

"But if you don't, you might lose both of them," the doctor emphasized. "We need to do this immediately; time is no more on our side." He begged my grandmother whose spirit was already dampened by the news. She unconsciously ignored the doctor in her state of thoughtfulness.

Mama called for the doctor. She wanted an assurance of her baby's safety at least and was ready to barter her life for mine.

"I will do everything within my ability to save both of you, Oludayo," he assured her. Mama agreed to sign the consent form and she was swiftly taken to the operation room right after. Grandma tried to follow but the theatre was out of bounds. She waited in the hallway like she had waited the past long nine months.

"Eni tí àn úngbé Ìyàwó bòwà bá...Kì hí Yo orùn" *A husband expecting his wife does not have to stretch his neck, the wife is coming anyways*-the Caucasian doctor said as he closed the door behind him. It was surprising he could speak fluent *Yoruba*.

Grandma found the telephone exchange office and made several calls to Daddy's office to ask how far he was from reaching Egbe.

As the clock struck 11:05 AM in the morning of the first day of December 1997, the squeal of a newcomer, pulled from its amniotic habitat, broke the stillness of the harmattan morning. I was carefully pulled out of my mother's uterus and I kicked with the strength of a mule. But it was not until 6:00 PM that the 4 kg bundle was placed in my mother's arms. Her frail hands held me tenderly with the fear of crushing the treasure she had almost bartered her life for.

Jubilant tears rolled down her cheeks and wetted my body as she pressed down her face on me and doused my soft skin with doting kisses. She settled me on her bosom, and we melted together into one perfect form.

"The only justification for an endured pain is a favourable result, anything less is injustice."

Daddy's mother, Mrs. Eboade Ajenifuja, also waited patiently for the good news at the hospital. She arrived a few minutes after my mother was taken into the theatre. My paternal grandmother had heard about her fragile daughter-in-law and travelled 275 kms from Ibadan to Egbe to see her. Consequently, I did not last long in my mother's arms before I was passed around the many impatient hands that itched to hold the latest creation.

Grandma Feyisayo rubbed my mama's exhausted head and whispered endearments to her. When mama regained little strength, she embraced her mother-in-law and began telling her the troubles preceding the eventual blessings. How she woke up four days earlier with labour pains; the pain which grew gradually until that morning, when it got to the point where it was as if the atoms that made up the lower half of her body were being split in a nuclear reactor.

"The baby will not wait further; she wants to come out quickly," she said to my father when she called him very early at dawn.

"Let me have my bath and leave immediately for the bus park," he said. "What about the …"

"Nothing is more important than the birth of our child," Daddy cut in. He arrived at the hospital an hour after my birth.

After calling Daddy and getting her things in order, Mama and Grandma Feyisayo hired a taxi which took them to Omu-Aran General Hospital, where Mama had registered for antenatal care months earlier. The doctors at Omu-Aran had considered her condition too fragile to handle. They were not equipped for such complicated childbirth. So, she was referred to Ilorin General Hospital.

She could have ended up at Ilorin General Hospital, but some of the staff at Omu-Aran General Hospital who became her friends in her antenatal days, told her of a better choice at Egbe, at ECWA private hospital with White doctors. If White people put a man on the moon, then complicated childbirth should be a walk in the park for them.

*   *   *

BON ANNIVERSAIRE

My first birthday a year later was celebrated with fanfare in Abuja, but the next morning my parents drove to Omu-Aran with me to Iya Bolanle's house where I was initiated into the order of the women from Omu-Aran.

The news of this initiation reached my paternal grandmother Mama Eboade Ajenifuja, who found it sacrilegious and disrespectful as children are patrilineal in Yorubaland. She arrived in Omu-Aran unannounced and vented her displeasure. She charged around the room spitting fire, wondering who came up with the idea of female circumcision.

"How dare you do that to my granddaughter? How dare you do such to a year-old girl? This is barbarism," Grandma Eboade shouted.

But my parents saw nothing wrong with the procedure. Father explained to her how 'ikola' was a religious and cultural rite of passage, an everlasting covenant of the flesh between God and Abraham.

"All the people circumcised in the Bible were males. Have you read about any woman who was circumcised in the Bible?" Grandma blurted and stormed out of the room. No one could talk her into agreeing to female circumcision. She later came for me and cuddled me for a short while before returning to Ibadan, leaving a strong warning against circumcision of my yet-to-be-born siblings.

These two stories are the most monumental things which have happened to me until now, which were not under my control: the day I was born and the day I was circumcised. Everything else has had my input.

Wednesday 5th March, 2025
WHO IS ADEOLA?

As I opened the door of my childhood room at my parents' home, my reminiscences died away gradually like the last flame of burning paper.

I walked down the stairs to the living room, looked across and saw my father's friend Ada in the library section. She sat across from Daddy and they chatted pleasantly. She passed a book titled *Botany & Herbal Medicine* to my dad and she also had another copy of the same book.

I walked into the library and hugged my dad and looked towards her. Her eyes welcomed me. I went close and said, "I'm sorry, Ada, for the last time. I was truthfully under a lot of pressure. But it didn't warrant that I spoke to you like that."
She grabbed my hands, rubbed them in hers and looked into my eyes and spoke with compassion, "Adeola, God is my witness, I did not take offence. I know just how much strain you were under," she continued, beaming at me.

I could read unsaid things in her eyes and I knew that even if she felt offended then, she no longer harbored animosity towards me. With a big smile, I asked if I could share from her biscuit. I spotted a pack in her bag and it was my favourite shortbread produced in the UK. She reached in her bag and gave me half of the pack and I was even more convinced our scuffle was over. I returned to my room.

As I reached the door to my room, a thought in form of a question hit me with the force of a bullet. I stopped. In a similar manner as the Lord Jesus Christ, I found myself asking: "Who do people say I am?"
"Who is Adeola?"
"*Who* is Dr. Adeola Jemima Ajenifuja?"

In my case though, my mahogany door was my disciple. Even without anyone nearby to respond to me, asking that question was perhaps the most honest moment of my adult life. I had already examined my birth, so I decided to go forward a few years to Adeola, the teenager.

My teenage days were fun and moderate-I was a regular Nigerian teenager: I went to school, got good grades, and was active in church. I was a member of the choir at my parents' church, The Rock: The Christ Assembly Abuja Branch, along Airport Road.

I met Chukwuemeka Pahoose in church, the young chap with a chapter in life that led to my own. His family moved to Abuja from Anambra. I was fifteen, he was sixteen and I was instantly fascinated by him.

He was tall, light-skinned and had a birthmark on his left hand. Coincidentally, I had a birthmark too but on my right hand. He was friendly and open to everyone; he also did very well academically, and soon he became the leading teen in the teen ministry. He was charming, calm and cheerful.

Our first meaningful meeting was when the choir was looking for a lead singer for a solo scheduled for the coming Sunday service. *Chuks*-as I always called him-was selected. I asked to join the solo after we both tried for the part. The choirmaster was so impressed that he eventually turned it into a duet.

That Sunday, Chuks started the first verse. We both sang the chorus, then my verse came up. During my verse, he adlibbed and showed off his vocal dexterity and brought up some beautiful dance steps which animated our rendition, making it better than we practised. Then we took the last verse together.

When I moved left, he moved right. Then we did the *tap-tip* moves simultaneously like Buchi, the reggae gospel musician. After all, the song was Buchi's, titled *Bridegroom*. The church gave us a standing ovation after the performance.

We became close friends after that day and did stuff together. Chuks was very good to me and treated me like a queen. He always put me first in our friendship. He was kind, gentle and sweet.

We sat for the West African Senior School Certificate exam together. We were both in the science class in our respective schools. I attended a private secondary in Area 1, Abuja; he went to a public secondary school in Gwagwalada. In spite of the difference in our schools and status, we began to study together. One day as we did, I scooted over to him and covered his jaw with my hands. For the past weeks, I resisted the strong temptation to kiss him, but I couldn't resist anymore.

"Adeola, what are you doing?" he asked as he moved away from me.

"I..ehm…think I have feelings for you. I've been restraining myself from expressing how I feel about you for a while," I stammered.

"I can't do that with you, love is not in the cards for us. I am betrothed already, and I will marry her when I am out of school. I cannot love another," he said firmly.

"How can you be betrothed at this age and in these modern times?" I asked incredulously.

"Our parents have been friends from their childhood days and our fathers promised that their children would marry each other. Obianuju wasn't even born when I got betrothed to her. My father just betrothed me to the first daughter of her parents when I was born."

"This doesn't even make sense!" I said sternly, as my body jittered.

"Chukwuemeka Pahoose, I put it to you that you are lying," I continued.

He reached for a book in his schoolbag and extracted a picture from it. He gave me the picture, but I refused to take a look at it at first. I did eventually.

"This is Obianuju," he said as I turned my back to him. "I am required to carry her picture on me at all times. I barely know her as she lives in Port Harcourt, but I know I am required to marry her in the future, else my parents would disown me for breaking a sacred promise and causing them shame."

"Wait, Chukwuemeka, you are smarter than such bullocks you are packaging. I don't want to believe you actually take these things hook, line and sinker. It is very bland," I said in disbelief. I picked my bag, already feeling miffed by Chuks's hogwash.

"I am sorry, Adeola, this is a dilemma for me as well. I have feelings for you, yet I have to respect my parents' wishes. It is our tradition as *Anambrarians* and also, my parents are *Amadioha* worshippers. I am lucky to have access to church."

"You liar!" I cut in. "You just told me that you cannot love me. And what does it mean *'Anambrarians'*? I have never considered your tribe ever. It has never been a factor in our relationship."

He laughed involuntarily, but I felt the pain in his laughter.

"Adeola, I didn't say I do not love you. I said my feelings for you are useless," he clarified, shamefacedly.

"What's the difference?" I quizzed with a managed tempered.

"The difference is that regardless of what I actually feel, I cannot show you the love you deserve."

"You know what? I don't have to stay here and listen to this," I said as I slung my bag on my back and fled.

By Sunday, I ruminated on the situation and I knew he had no other choice than to do what his parents wanted. I placed myself in his shoes and realised what defying the Ajenifujas would cost me. It was unthinkable. Yet it felt wrong that two hearts meant for each other were prevented from expression due to differing ethnicity and cultural heritage.

We saw at church on that Sunday and he tried to give further explanation. I did not give the room. Instead, I hugged him and said in acceptance as I disengaged from his warmth, "I understand, Chuks. I do. I would rather lose and have you than win and lose you."

That afternoon, we gave our hearts to a platonic friendship even though we both wanted more. Chuks was my person; our feelings were mutual. He was my friend, my mentor, my benchmark. He was so dependable that I saw the world through his eyes. He sharpened me on some things, I sharpened him on others. We balanced each other, yet we could not quench our common desire. Even now than ever, *what would Chuks do*? is the ultimate question in navigating my decision to carry his child. He was everything to me. In him, excellence was *natuurlijk*. He lived by it, even in inadequacy. I desired him so much, but I could never have him. It seemed unfair, like a zugzwang.

"Watch but thou toucheth not, touch but thou biteth not, bite but thou swalloweth not."

"Death took a huge treasure when it touched down on Chukwuemeka Pahoose," I mused as I heard a knock on my bedroom door.

It was my mother who came to tell me dinner was ready. She made my favourite food-pounded yam and *efo-riro*. I settled at the dining table to enjoy my meal.

"Who is Dr. Adeola Jemima Ajenifuja?" you ask.

I guess I cannot define myself without a touch of Chukwuemeka Pahoose. I am equally sure if he looked back from the afterlife, he would not be able to remove me from his memory. It is a blessing to carry his progeny. It gladdens me that a part of him gestates in my belly.

There is more about Dr. Adeola Jemima Ajenifuja, but for now I have to devour this delicacy-a miniature mountain of pounded yam and *efo-riro* to be brought to nought.

My name is Adeola Jemima Ajenifuja and this is my story.

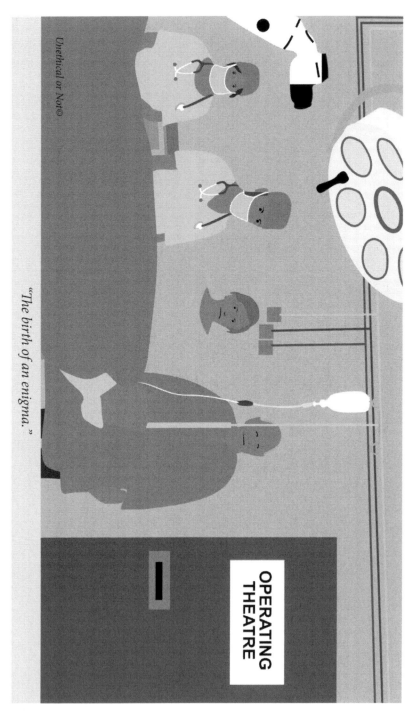

"The birth of an enigma."

8. Acts, Laws & Legislations

" ——————————

A nation that mishandles the health of its people is sick from the top down. She is a republic of dead men walking."

8. Acts, Laws & Legislations

"A nation that mishandles the health of its people is sick from the top down. She is a republic of dead men walking."

10.00 AM
Thursday 13th March, 2025

PROFESSOR LEVI

It was my sixth appearance in court. My friends and family members were in attendance, including my brother's fiancée Lade-Iwalewa invited her from London. So far it appeared my court appearances were getting over as ruling on my case approached. Perhaps I'd appear in court for another one or two times. I had lined up my last witness for that day: Prof. Bilha Zelda Levi. There was an undeniable reckoning that the lead prosecutor, Mr. Tundu Wada Gida, did not have any more witnesses. So, we had that appearance and the closing arguments. Judgement would be read on a set date depending on the Judge's decision.

We all sat and waited in the courtroom for another spectacle even if we were gradually in the anticlimactic moments. Ms. Olabamiji, my counsel, sat beside me, dressed elegantly and looking stunningly beautiful. Judge Amaradi asked for my final witness. He looked very stern and a little preoccupied. I wondered what was on his mind.

"I call to the stand Prof. Bilha Zelda Levi," I said briskly as I left my seat.

Bailiff Aguntasolo brought in Prof. Levi and swore her in with a **Quran**.

I looked in Gida's corner and observed the countenances of Chukwuemeka's parents. I had seen them earlier but gave nary attention to them. They looked frazzled and unenergetic. Then I walked up to Prof. Levi in the witness stand with a neutral smile on my face. "Good morning, Prof," I said.

"Good morning, doc," she replied.

"Please, can you introduce yourself to the members of the jury."

She coughed quietly to clear her throat. "Well, my name is Prof. Mrs. Bilha Zelda Levi. I am an Israeli citizen married to a Nigerian. I am a professor in reproductive medicine with decades of experience. I obtained my bachelor's degree in medicine and surgery from the University of South Liverpool, United Kingdom. I underwent my residency in my home country of Israel where I specialised in gynaecology. I met my husband during my residency; he was undergoing his own residency in thoracic medicine. We fell in love and got married. When he was returning to his country after his residency, I came with him."

"You moved to another country for love," I asked.

"Yes," she said with a succulent smile.

"We moved to Nigeria about twenty-one years ago and I continued my practice here, deciding to specialise in IVF. I became a professor a few years later and I am the current Head of the Abuja Institute of Reproductive Science, AIRS, a state-of-the-art private IVF clinic cum training school." She paused and looked at me and I nodded to encourage her to go on.

"I am also a member of the Board of Nigerian Society for Reproductive Medicine, NSRM," she continued.

"What does your job entail as head of an IVF unit?" I asked.

"As head of a private IVF clinic, the primary elements of my job are as follows. One, to ensure there is a Total Quality Management System for every process in our clinic. Two, to ensure there is perfect collaboration between the medical and laboratory teams. And three, to ensure each member of the organisation is conversant with the Standard Operating Procedure of each process. All processes are deemed important and nothing is too small to be left to chance. The employee in charge of stand-by generators is as important and responsible for the success of the process as the head of the clinic. A one-hour power cut can be disastrous to developing embryos in our incubators. Finally, my work means I ensure the marketing team is working hard to strategize better in recruiting more patients.

"In the end, my job requires that I coordinate activities to ensure our collective input results in expected or even better output. An output of happy pregnant patients and satisfied non-pregnant patients. Essentially, we want satisfied clients irrespective of the outcome of their treatments."

"Thank you, Prof. Levi," I said. "May I ask what role you play as a member of Nigerian Society for Reproductive Medicine?"

"Well, I am a member of the board, which is the final decision-maker of the body. Our role has been to maintain global best practices in all aspects of our operations: informed consent; standard and reasonable pricing and costings of IVF treatment; safe and certified consumables and products used in practice; good salary ranges and pay scale for doctors, nurses, clinical embryologists, and other support staff; as well as ensure ethical guidelines for both private and public IVF clinics.

"But in all sincerity, it is a herculean task. We have major challenges with government support in this field of science. With a population of 300 million people in 2025, the government does not invest resources in the field. The Senate is not open to discussing or approving laws to protect patients or the practitioners."

"Objection, my Lord," LP Gida interrupted, startling me and Prof. Levi.

"My Lord, Prof. Levi is not required to provide information on questions not asked. She is not an expert in Nigerian politics or governance or economy," LP Gida said.

I stole a glance at Ms. Olabamiji and she nodded as a sign for me to challenge Gida's objection.

"My Lord, Prof. Levi is indeed an expert in this area and is conversant with both extant and missing laws in the field. She has a bird's-eye view of how the practice is done in developed countries. So, I beg the court to allow this line of questioning and answers. Otherwise we would be required to fly in a foreign expert. Prof. Bilha Zelda Levi has seen the two sides of the coin and is competent and fit to throw light on this," I submitted.

Judge Amaradi took a moment, then spoke briefly.

"While this is not exactly our usual practice, for the sake of perspective, I will allow this line of enquiry just a little longer. It might help the jurors to gain clarity as this is an unfamiliar territory to most, if not all of us."

"My Lord, with utmost respect to your Lordship and your courtroom, this line of questioning is prejudiced against the state," LP Gida replied.

"I note your objection, but I will allow this to go on for a few more minutes. Dr. Ajenifuja, please, finish up with Prof. Levi," Judge Amaradi said.

"Thank you, my Lord. Prof. Levi, please, continue," I said.

"As I was saying, there are no laws passed by the government to regulate the practice. As I speak to you right now, there are IVF clinics here in Nigeria that allow up to seven embryos to be replaced back in the uterus. Highly unconscionable, right?"

"Objection!" LP Gida cut in again. "My Lord, we are going beyond the scope of the case."

"Objection overruled," Judge Amaradi said.

"So, are you saying each IVF clinic in different parts of this country makes its own rules and laws?" I asked Prof. Levi.

"Indeed," she replied.

"So, a dead, important member of a family, a friend who dies by accident can be operated on and have his testicular materials collected and cryopreserved on his behalf in Nigeria without a law to stop such activity?" I asked.

"There is no law. Not even a freaking Act in place to control anything. There is nothing to protect the patients or anybody really. So yes, it is possible. The samples will, however, be kept in quarantine until the infection screening status of the original bearer of the testicular material is determined," she explained.

"My Lord, the court has given Dr. Ajenifuja too much room," LP Gida interjected in a raised voice which carried more vexation than courtesy.

"I'm done, the witness is yours," I said calmly and walked away, cutting off his tirade.

"I have only one question for you, Prof Levi," LP Gida said in a clipped tone. "What law do you follow in your clinic?"

Prof. Levi paused before speaking. "Well I was trained in the UK and in Israel, so I follow the Human Fertilization and Embryology (HFEA) Act guidelines. HFEA is domiciled in the UK and has one of the most stringent laws around the world. There are countries in Europe though with less stringent laws. Belgium has one of the most accommodating laws in Europe. There, human embryos can be generated for research purposes after approval by an ethics panel. In European countries such as Germany, Italy and even in the UK, there is lesser accommodation compared to Belgium. USA also has less stringent laws. But truthfully, we do not have any Act of the National Assembly or state legislatures on Assisted Reproduction practices in Nigeria. Is this not worrisome enough?"

"Thank you, that's enough," LP Gida said in a resigned tone.

I smirked in my seat.

Prof. Levi had let the cat out.

"My Lord, I will like to ask one more question," Mr. Gida said.

I imagined what one more question was left in his pouch of antagonism.

"Prof. Levi, are you suggesting that we become lawless and practise anyhow: since there are no laws, we can do anything we want?" LP Gida asked.

"No," she answered briskly. "I am saying, you should make laws around this field. And let any breach of it be punishable by sanction. Let everything be in black and white. We do not create a new law out of thin air. To adjudicate, you have to create laws and commensurate penalties for infractions"

"What about the 'Do No Harm' principle, which is the cornerstone of the Hippocratic Oath-does it not apply in this case? Is that oath not being broken by the actions of Dr. Ajenifuja?"

"What about it? Harm can only really be done to the living and in this case, Engr. Pahoose was already dead. Therefore, the Hippocratic Oath does not apply."

"Thank you, Prof. Levi. I have no further questions for this witness, my Lord," Mr. Gida said to Judge Amaradi with disappointment written all over his face.

"You can step down, Prof. Levi. Thank you," Judge Amaradi said.

Bailiff Aguntasolo helped her out of the witness box and she walked back to her seat in the middle of the courtroom.

"Thank you all, this case has been adjourned for the closing arguments and the jury's verdict in two weeks from today," Justice Amaradi said and ended the day's proceedings.

My family and I hugged one another. We looked towards the Pahoose family and saw a quiet air of disappointment on their faces. I felt a little sad for them, but I couldn't be remorseful; I knew the only thing that would make them happy was to see me in jail and my pregnancy terminated.

My name is Adeola Jemima Ajenifuja and this is my story.

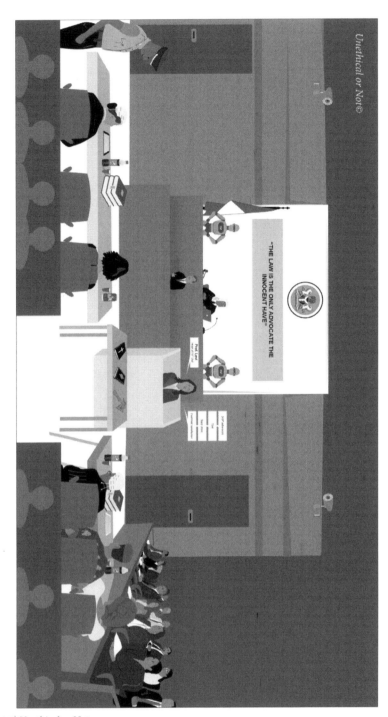

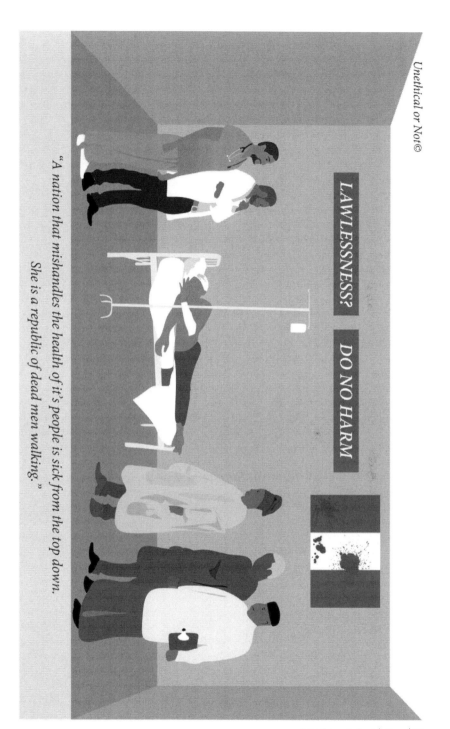

LAWLESSNESS?

DO NO HARM

"A nation that mishandles the health of it's people is sick from the top down.

She is a republic of dead men walking."

9. The Verdict

"The will to fight opposition dies quickly at the realisation that, sometimes, the justice system is unjust."

9. The Verdict

"The will to fight opposition dies quickly at the realisation that, sometimes, the justice system is unjust."

5:00 AM
Thursday 27th March, 2025

APPREHENSION

I woke up early by 5:00 AM. on the D-Day, when the judicial antagonism between me and Gida would be settled. The jurors had heard all sides of the argument. Our closing argument had little impact on the possible ruling, but Ms. Olabamiji and I rehearsed well and went over keywords that could tilt the jury's verdict in my favour. Since the hearings began, I had not imagined what the outcome would be. I had not imagined being found guilty and the consequence of such ruling. I could be found guilty of medical malpractice, and a compulsory abortion demanded. And setting me free could set a precedence for unruly behaviour in medical practice.

I imagined the members of the jury in a dusty room. All served *akara* and bread with Pepsi-Cola drinks, arguing on top of their voices, their energy focused on the desecration of the dead. Disrespect of the departed. All coming to the conclusion that I had done wrong.

We arrived at the courthouse and saw a coterie of journalists camped at the entrance. We were not prepared for the large number.

Earlier in the case, LP Gida used the press against me but since the gag order from the Judge, he desisted. Because of the same gag order, I had not given any radio or TV station access to me for a story or discussion about my case. I encountered a few newsmen during my appearances but not this assemblage of news stations prepared to go live during the proceedings. Was the Judge aware? It would throw me off balance and affect my closing argument. I asked Ms. Olabamiji and she told me it wasn't impossible to get the newsmen out. That Judge Amaradi did not entertain theatrics in his courtroom.

On one side were people with placards shouting, "Desecrator!" "Find her guilty!" On the other side were placards, held high, that bore words like "Unethical," "Betrayer," "Unlawful," and "Inhumane." One really got to me; it said, "Ugly." For a second, I laughed *in italics*.

We stepped out of the car and hurried towards the entrance. The journalists hurried along with us. A peek at a TV from a distance confirmed they were live. Thanks to Iwalewa, who cleared the path for us and we made it inside.

The courtroom was full.

I looked at Ms. Olabamiji. "This is crazy. I thought you said there weren't going to be theatrics?"

"I promise you, Dr. Ajenifuja, the courtroom will be cleared to ensure you have a comfortable environment," she said, and we walked to our usual seats. Ms. Olabamiji excused herself to speak with the court clerk. She spoke and gesticulated towards the crowd. The clerk looked and seemed concerned. He disappeared into the Judge's chambers and returned ten minutes later.

He came to us and said Judge Amaradi told him he would clear the court when he came in.

I became more comforted. In the direction of LP Gida were Chukwuemeka's parents regaled in typical Igbo attire. Mr Gida spoke inaudibly as though he was rehearsing his closing argument. The clerk called the court in order and announced the arrival of the Judge.

Judge Amaradi took his seat and pulled his microphone closer. "Before I bring in the jury, I need to clear the courtroom. I need only the families and friends of the two sides in my courtroom."

Bailiff Aguntasolo and his colleagues cleared the room. By the time they were done, we were less than twenty people in the room.

CLOSING ARGUMENTS

Mr Gida began his closing argument. "There is an oath in medical practice only found in that line of profession. Engineers, lawyers, pharmacists, biochemists are bound by ethics. It is only in medicine that a doctor is required to do no harm at all times. Even in times of war, he is obliged to do no harm. Dr. Adeola Jemima Ajenifuja has done exactly the opposite. She has turned the mourning of the Pahoose family into a sourer one. Beyond medical malpractice, she is pregnant with a child in a very abominable way. A pregnancy we ask the court to terminate. To make an example of her for such atrocities. We ask that she spends time behind bars.

"She might say she has rights. But her decision to take any matters into her hands considering extracting sperm cells from the corpse of Engr.Chukwuemeka Titus Pahoose to impregnate herself should have gone before the court before it was acted out. I, therefore, find Dr. Adeola Jemima Ajenifuja's act as criminal. Let the jury pass its verdict to put her behind the iron bars. If the jury does not do its duty, I fear that she would be let back into the society to spread her abominable ideas to right-thinking citizens of the Federal Republic of Nigeria."

Chukwuemeka's parents nodded in agreement from their seats.

Then came my turn to speak. Ms. Olabamiji looked at me with cheers of confidence.

I walked to the floor, then began.

"The day Engr. Chukwuemeka Titus Pahoose died was the longest day of my life. I received a call from his phone by a bystander who saw him go down, telling me my friend was dead. She had dialled the last number on his call log, which was mine. I rushed to the scene and held Chukwuemeka in my hands. He was already dead. Two minutes later, an EMT ambulance arrived and we rushed him to Abuja Municipal Hospital where I worked. Our journey to the hospital took fifteen minutes, enough time for me to be Chukwuemeka's proxy. I was in shock for the first ten minutes of the journey. But within the last five minutes, I recalled that the content of his will gave me sole power of attorney on issues regarding his health-to observe his Do Not Resuscitate (DNR) choice and to take custody of his corpse, if death came earlier. That will of testament was made available to this court and has been confirmed valid at the Nigerian Court of Will and Testaments.

"One thing is clear: most people do not have what Chukwuemeka and I had. We were broken up and prevented from being together because of a tradition that is four hundred years old. A tradition that forces a child to choose whom to be in love with and marry only from his clan. A tradition that predisposes *Anambrarians* to chromosomal aberration-of having the likelihood to bear offspring with deformities. Something Charles Darwin's offspring suffered from because he married his first cousin. Chukwuemeka wanted out of this traditional practice, yet he remained in it out of respect for his parents. Parents that later disowned him for only breaking a fraction of a family tradition. The sad part was he only asked for a little help.

"Everyone needs a little help sometimes. Even my father needs a little help sometimes. Yet he is one of the richest inventors in Nigeria.

"So, Chukwuemeka was disowned and ex-communicated from the Pahoose family. For what? For getting help from me. Just a little money. And because the Pahoose family is a proud one, they gave up their only child. They were cajoled to file a suit against me by the Lead Prosecutor's office. A suit to prevent me from bringing a child of Engr. Chukwuemeka Pahoose to this world. The suit aims to present me as a criminal, invalidate me, and get the Medical Society of Nigeria to withdraw my license. Is this an ethnic war between the Igbo and Yoruba people? I beseech you jury to find me not guilty of the charges against me as there is still no law set against my actions. None set up by the Medical Society of Nigeria, the Nigerian Society for Reproductive Medicine, nor by the Nigerian constitution. I broke no law. Therefore, I should be acquitted and set free from any encumbrance whatsoever."

I spoke and walked back to my seat.

Justice Amaradi announced the end for all matters on the case. He looked towards the jury and spoke. "We have been on this case for the past two months or even more. Today, however, it comes to an end. Ladies and gentlemen of the jury, what is your verdict on the case set before this court? I urge objectivity and fairness.

"The court shall be in recess for a consensus amongst you. The court is in recess now and the defence and Mr. Gida should hang around the court area for when we will bring in the jury."

I became a little apprehensive. "I need some space," I said to my family as I looked around. I exited the courtroom for a few minutes. My family members stepped out too; they all went towards their cars.

Jumoke and Ms. Olabamiji stayed with me.

There was a shop painted in Pepsi ads. I entered it to get myself a cold bottle of Pepsi and *puff-puff*.

I asked Jumoke and Ms. Olabamiji if they wanted something.

No, they chorused. They stood about six metres away from the shop.

I stood in front of a young vendor. She brought my order and collected five hundred naira. Then a man approached me. He was of average height, dark, and estimated to be within my age brackets. He smiled at me and said hi. I found a seat and looked away from him and focused on Jumoke and Ms. Olabamiji.

He repeated his greetings by saying, "How are you, madam?"

"I am not interested in talking to a journalist," I answered him.

"I'm not one," he said. "All the journalists have been driven out of the court compound. A gag order was issued with a fine of one million naira and a jail term."

I looked around and discovered indeed that no one was harassing me.

"In all fairness, I have been following your case and I am fascinated by it. My name is Francis Okiemute. I am a statistician. I handle major private and government data across the country. I like you very much."

I laughed for some seconds, like I was pumped with dinitrogen oxide gas I didn't ask for, water rolling down my face. I had not laughed like that since I began court appearances. The new Mr. Francis had shock on his face.

Then I said with the remnant of a chuckle in my throat, "I am sorry to respond like that. How could you be attracted to someone like me, even in my predicament? I am almost set to become a criminal. lose my license and credibility."

"I understand your situation and as I said, I have been following your case. In my entire being, I have never seen a love so selfless like yours. Giving it all to Engr. Pahoose. I imagine an opportunity to be given just a bit of that affection. Say, ten per cent? I will gladly and wholeheartedly take it."

"You know I am six months pregnant, right?"

"Of course, I am aware. I am willing to be a part of you guys. Be a family. Even as a second-class citizen in your kingdom."

"What if I am found guilty?" I said.

"I will fight for you. Burn the whole forest for you, to gain your freedom."

Ms. Olabamiji and Jumoke waved to get my attention. "The jury is back," they hollered.

I ran speedily, then turned to wave at Francis, who spoke in a thunderous voice that echoed through the walls of the courthouse: "The win is yours. I will be here waiting for you."

I smiled and turned to have another look at him. Then I realised we did not exchange contacts. He looked cool and I had not dated in a while. I jettisoned the thought from my mind and focussed on the matter at hand.

I made it to Jumoke and Ms. Olabamiji. We immediately proceeded into the courtroom.

MADAM FOREPERSON

My family was already in, sitting in their usual position. I asked Ms. Olabamiji why the jury came back so early. "It could be good or bad," she answered. But there was optimism in her voice.

It had not been an hour yet.

The court clerk called the court to order and Judge Amaradi took his seat.

The members of the jury entered and took their respective seats.

Judge Amaradi asked the foreperson: "Madam Foreperson, I have been told you have reached a verdict on this case."

She stood up and said, "Yes, Your Honour, we have."

A sheet of paper was given to bailiff Aguntasolo, who in turn gave it to Judge Amaradi.

The Judge took a look and gave it back to bailiff Aguntasolo, who gave it back to the foreperson. "Dr. Adeola Adenifuja, please, rise for the verdict," the Judge commanded. "Madam Foreperson, you can read your verdict for the defence and the court to hear."

Madam Foreperson spoke: "On the matter of the State against Dr. Adeola Jemima Ajenifuja: 1. For committing medical malpractice, we find in favour of the state. 2. On the matter of usage of the gamete of the dead for impregnation, we find in favour of the state."

The atmosphere in the courtroom from the side of the Pahoose' rumbled mildly with triumph.

It was like I had lost the bones in my body as I had a free fall to my seat.

Then Judge Amaradi cut in. "Based on the law of the country and the will of testament that Dr. Ajenifuja has provided, I hereby issue a JNOV-judgement notwithstanding the verdict. If there are no laws to prevent posthumous usage of gametes in the land, there is, therefore, a need for such law to be created. A bill needs to be passed by the Senate. As of today, 27th March 2025, there is no such law. The state could have brought a case of desecration of the dead body against Dr. Adeola, which carries a fine and possibly a light sentence. But that was not the case in this situation. This case was not about morality. It was not about Dr. Adeola being UNETHICAL OR NOT. It is about if a law has been broken. I see no law broken here.

"On the two counts, I, therefore, find Dr. Adeola Jemima Ajenifuja not-guilty and declare her free to go back to her practice and I wish her the best with her pregnancy."

Judge Amaradi slammed the gavel and the court was dismissed.

My family and I were in shock, confused and exhilarated. We hugged one another for several minutes, crying with joy.

As we exited the court, I sighted Francis smiling. He hung at a corner of the front of the courthouse.

"I believed you were going to win. I never had a doubt." He walked with us to the car. My parents signalled me with their eyes to ask who Francis was. Even Jumoke and Ms. Olabamiji who already saw that I chatted with him before the verdict wanted to know.

Iwalewa, as well wanted to know who Francis was.

I looked at Francis who was beaming. I rubbed my hand on my belly as though I was about to make a statement and said to every awaiting prey of gossip and gist, "Well, this is Francis . . . ehm . . ."

He cut in and said, "Francis, Francis Okiemute is my name. We briefly met when the court went for recess earlier today."

"How did you know the verdict?" I asked.

"I have my contacts in this courthouse," he said proudly.

My parents looked at him unimpressed.

"Are you sure you are not a journalist?"

He became meek, seeing he said something fishy. "Oh no, I promise, I am not a journalist. I was simply interested in your case and found a legal way to follow its progress."

Everyone headed to the garage and I was left with Francis. Ms. Olabamiji hugged me and said congratulations before she departed.

"What do you want with me, Mr. Okiemute?" I asked.

He walked closer to me. I had the patience and the restfulness needed to evaluate his looks even more.

"I like you, Dr. Ms. Adeola Jemima Ajenifuja. You are like a superhero. A real-life superhero. We have seen Black Panther of Wakanda, we have seen Captain Marvel. We have seen Wonder Woman, we have seen Thor, Captain America, Iron Man, Supergirl, Superman. All of them are not real. None of them is real. Here we are with a Nigerian superhero. Or a super heroine? A heroine without a cape, with flesh and blood. Because of your case, the Senate would have to create new **Acts, Legislations and laws** in Assisted Reproductive Technology, as well as general medicine," he said.

"But in a way, I was sort of unethical; or maybe not. Is that not supposed to be a bad thing?" I said and walked towards our car.

"Either way. You are the reason we would have this change."

"I have to go with my family now."

"Can I have your number?". He asked

"You can get it from your contacts in the court, can't you?"

"I would like you to give it to me." He demanded gentlemanly

"Well, here's to stressing you: search for it like an explorer searches for crude oil."

"This is 2025, crude oil is already phasing out. But I get your drift."

We reached the garage, close to my father's bulletproof jeep. I looked at Francis, then gave him my business card.

He swiftly brought his out and handed it to me. He jumped and danced a gentle *shaku shaku* as he walked away. He headed towards the left-wing of the garage and opened his car with a voice command and got in. It was a **Jaguar S-type, 2024 model**. He did some more dance moves with his upper body as he sat in his car. I heard his playful laughter.

I laughed involuntarily at his puerility, but it was a beautiful sight to behold after the weight of the recent months.

I joined my family in the car and Iwalewa drove off.

Francis' car came behind us. He veered to the left and waved as though he saw me checking on him.

We got home and Lade came to hug me tightly. She held my hand and we both walked into my father's library. "I am elated for your victory," she said to me. "You have always been a source of strength and encouragement to me. I am always proud to talk to my friends about you even before your case. Your view of life is enigmatic and heroic. You have never shown any weakness. Something I see in Iwalewa, too. I love you, sis, and will hope you visit us soon in London. Iwalewa and I return to London next week; our holiday is almost exhausted for the year."

"Thank you, sister-in-law, too. I fell in love with you at first sight. I knew after a few days with you that you would fit perfectly well into the family. Your love for my brother and humanity is exceptional. The great work you do is mind-blowing. I will surely miss you. I am sure you will come for my baby dedication."

"Of course, we will; we will not miss it for the world."

We hugged one more time.

"What are you going do with Francis?" she asked. "I see chemistry plus arithmetic between the two of you. I pray he is a good guy."

I bowed my head like an Oriental woman in affirmation. We joined the family for dinner.

A TOAST

Everyone was at the dinner: my parents, Iwalewa, Lade, Jumoke, Dr. Opeoluwa Adewumi, Dr. Omidan Tiwatope, Ada, Ms. Olabamiji.

As the dinner ended, we shared a glass of wine each. I stood up and announced I had something to say. "I would like to express my gratitude to my family and friends. Daddy, Mummy, Iwalewa, Lade, Jumoke, Ada and everyone else sitting at this table. It is seen and observed across cultures and traditions that sometimes blood is just blood and water is just water. There is no need to compare the two. No need to say: blood is thicker than water. Because families betray each other sometimes. They can pull each other down. They can commit the worst atrocities, like they don't know one another. Like they don't share DNA, like sharing a surname doesn't mean anything. But I am lucky that my entire family supported me from day one. They never, for once, found fault in my choice. They followed me anywhere I went, one hundred per cent behind me. Maybe it had to do with the training they gave me, maybe not. Maybe it was because they trusted my judgement or maybe not. One thing is surely clear: they stood by me. I am grateful. I am grateful to the Ajenifujas, my in-laws to be, my friends and every acquaintance I gained along the way. I could not ask for a better family, better friends and acquaintances. I love you all and will always be there for you, too. A toast to a good life ahead."

In the end, we listened and danced to some music from Brymo's collections: *Alajo Somolu, Something Good, Purple Jar, Grand Papa* and many more. My name is Adeola Jemima and this is my story.

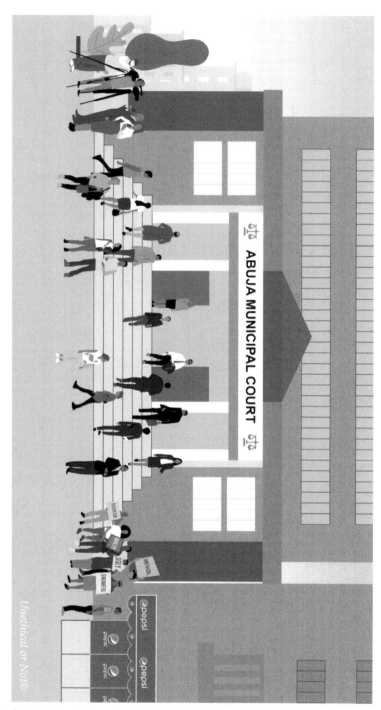

Unethical or Not©

"THE LAW IS THE ONLY ADVOCATE THE
INNOCENT HAVE"

10. A New Dawn

" ―――――――――――――
In all, love can be found in the most mysterious place."

10. A New Dawn

"In all, love can be found in the most mysterious place."

3:20 PM
Saturday
12th April, 2025

A DATE

After about two weeks, Francis invited me to a lunch date and I accepted. The place was at McDonald's along Ajose Adeogun, Abuja Central Area. When we met, he hugged me carefully as my belly was already the shape of a large watermelon. He pulled a chair for me to sit. An iPad was in our front for us to place orders. The AI system was topnotch. I ordered chicken nuggets, triple cheeseburger and banana milkshake. He ordered crispy chicken, bacon salad and vanilla milkshake. After eight minutes, a courteous robot brought our orders. "Hi, Dr. Adeola Ajenifuja," it said, "Here is your order of chicken nuggets, triple cheeseburger, and banana milkshake. Hi, Mr. Francis Okiemute, let me create a space on your table to keep your order of crispy chicken, bacon salad and vanilla milkshake."

It lifted Francis' ipad, motioned to collect his bag, and put the tablet in it.

We started eating and talked in between.

"What do you find spectacular about me?" I asked him.

He slowly swallowed what was in his mouth and spoke. "Revolutionary! Revolutionary! Revolutionary! That is what you are. You changed the game in major areas. The laws are getting changed because of Dr. Adeola Jemima Ajenifuja. People respect women's choice and place in our society more now. You know the interesting thing about it?"

I said, no.

"You did not put a label on it. Something as striking as that, yet you never gave it a name. Above all, the trust and chemistry between you and Chukwuemeka Titus Pahoose-it's an unusual gift that happens to us just once, if it does. I have never seen any couple that very trusting of each other. I was shocked to realise you were never even married to each other."

I nodded in agreement.

"So, if I could get a taste of that. If you could give me ten per cent of what you and Engr. Pahoose had, it will be more than satisfying."

"You know, I am pregnant for him. Are you comfortable with that?" I said

"In this time and age, the world sees things differently now. Families are uniting into beautiful relations in spite of not sharing DNA. I want you. All I ask is that you let me in," he said with devotion in his eyes.

I reached and touched his hand to calm his appetite for me, and said, "Okay. It's 2025. Let's do this."

He stood up excitedly, came close and kissed me on my cheek.

I smiled as he sat back in his seat.

"I think we should quickly finish our food before they get cold," I said.

After the lunch, Francis offered to drive me in his **Jagz**. The interior of the 2024 S-type model was sophisticatedly furnished. It had a driverless feature and could follow a driver's lead. The sitting arrangement was spun round like in a spaceship.

Francis asked for my postcode. When I told him, he voice-commanded the GPS of the car.

"**Jagz**, drive us to ABV 10," he ordered.

"Why is the car barely making any sound?" I asked.

"It runs on water." he answered.

"Water?"

He said, "Well it runs on hydrogen gotten from the electrolysis of water." That he had a hydrogen station at home where he fueled the car with hydride, a form of hydrogen in a stable state. When needed to drive the engine, the hydride converts to hydrogen.

I was impressed. "How do you know so much about such technology," I asked. He told me he was a climate change warrior.

By this time, we had gotten closer to my house.

"Thank you for a good time today, Francis. I enjoyed every bit of it," I said.

He came closer, planted a wet kiss on my lips and said, "I want all of you Adeola. I want everything you are, merged to me. We will be great together."

I had not had a French kiss in a long time. I savoured its aftertaste on my lips and looked dumbfoundedly at him. He appeared to want more, so I buried my body in his chest; and traced his lips with mine. For minutes we remained in that incarnation till we disengaged. After that day, we saw regularly, for dinner and other things, enjoying blissfulness together.

When I was eight months and two weeks pregnant, he asked my hand in marriage.

I never expected we would grow together to want that and thought we were just having a great time. Plus, there was another man's baby in the picture.

"Life is not always a straight line. In a million years, I could never imagine wanting to marry a woman carrying another man's baby. I doubt if it is acceptable in my village. I doubt if my family agrees on such. One thing is crystal though. More than clear even, like broad daylight. As clear as snow in the land of the Eskimos. Like walking in the woods, getting saturated by the excess release of oxygen by trees. The clearance of head you get when your body is calm, rested, composed and hyper-oxygenated. I am clear about the situation and want this for myself, for your baby that will be our baby and the ones we will add as his or her siblings." He said.

"Adeola Jemima Ajenifuja, DNA could be a deal-breaker for some. It is not for me. My love for you exceeds DNA. I am in love with you and would want to spend the rest of my life with you." He rested.

I started crying uncontrollably. Then I hugged and kissed him.

"I have never seen any man care less about the societal implications of a choice this huge," I said. "At least not in the Nigerian society where stigmatisation of people like me can last forever. Thank you so much for loving me. I have grown to love you, too. I accept your proposal, to be your partner, your wife, your friend and the mother of all the children we could ever have. Though I do not want more than three kids."

We both laughed and he commented saying, "Three is a good number to stop."

We sealed the deal with a long pleasurable kiss.

*   *   *

NUCLEAR

Everyone came. From far and wide. Wito and Margot came from Belgium. Iwalewa, Lade, Jumoke, Omidan, Opeoluwa and Ada. I was already eight months and two weeks pregnant. The wedding was lavish and glorious.

Five days later, we had a baby shower. As we celebrated, my water broke and I was rushed to the hospital. I had a baby girl. We christened her with Chukwuemeka's last name as her middle name. Francis agreed to name her Abiola Pahoose Okiemute. Abiola grew to resemble Chukwuemeka. The Pahoose family attempted a visit to see Abiola, but we did not grant it.

"In a lost battle against a defendant, the plaintiff should not be granted a second chance; the defendant risks losing this time."

By the time Abiola was two years old, I was pregnant again. My work demanded we move to Lagos. There we had two more children, Akeju and Kalu.

My name is Adeola Jemima Ajenifuja and this is the end of the beginning of my story.

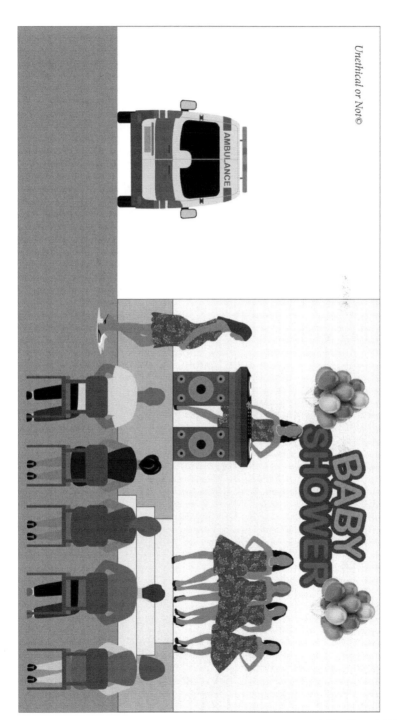

Your Support

You are at this page because you have digested the entire chapters of *Unethical Or Not*. The stories are a collection of true events, extrapolations of imaginative fictions and a heavy touch on a representation of a forward-thinking African's dream towards the achievement of great feats.

Writing this book started out simply to tell a story, but it grew into a piece that brought home for me a long-coveted vision. The vision to build Africa's foremost research and innovations development university called Qualitech-Vibrand University (QV University).

This vision has inspired me to give 50% of the profit from this book towards building QV University.

Your exchange of money for this work of literature is indirectly an investment into the future advancement of technologies and innovations in Nigeria and other African countries.

If you wish to support us, below is our organisation's details to make donations.

Thank you.

BANK(NIGERIA) ●—● **BANK(EU)**

BANK NAME: Diamond Bank/Access Bank

ACCOUNT HOLDER : Oluwasegun Babatunde

ACCOUNT NAME: Qualitech-Vibrand University

SORT CODE : 23-14-70

ACCOUNT NUMBER: 0102052359

ACCOUNT NUMBER :70279830

IBAN : GB04 TRWI 2314 7070 2798 30

PAYPAL

OUR PAYPAL ACCOUNT:

qvuniversitypaypal@gmail.com

Segun Babatunde

OLUWASEGUN, BABATUNDE

EDITORS
1. Ezenwa Ada
2. Terver Asongo
3. Immanuel James Ibe-anyanwu

MODEL
Mary Owusu
as "Dr.Adeola Jemima Ajenifuja."

DESIGNER
Charles Fate (Notch Designs)

EXECUTIVE PRODUCER
Oluwasegun Babatunde

Published by
STORIBUD LIMITED
Company number :12972092
Wa7 1JF
High Street,
Runcorn, United Kingdom

Printed in Great Britain
by Amazon

58215439R00071